Chef Daniel

The mystery of the Fendant sauce

By

Mylène THURRE-GEX

Book 1

Originally published in Switzerland in 2017

Copyright © 2022 Mylène Thurre-Gex

Cover picture: YAPA Photo, 1926 Fully, Switzerland

ISBN: 9798646152887

CONTENTS

DEDICATION...4

ACKNOWLEDGEMENTS.................................4

FENDANT WINE...5

DESCRIPTION OF THE PENTALOGY 6

MAIN CHARACTERS..................................7

CHARACTERS BY APPEARANCE...............8

EPILOGUE...240

ABOUT THE AUTHOR.............................244

ALSO BY MYLÈNE THURRE-GEX.........245

DEDICATION

To Johana and Florian
My niece and my nephew

To the Perkins and Marsden families who heartily
welcomed me in Brixton as an au pair.

ACKNOWLEDGEMENTS

To Marie-Claire and Muriel for their support.

To Jean-Paul, my brother, for his information about
Shanghai, China.

To Susan Ann Mellor for proof-reading this English
version.

FENDANT WINE

Fendant is a Chasselas wine from Switzerland. First introduced to the southern part of the country, Valais, in 1850, it has been protected there since 1966. No other winegrowing region has the right to use this appellation. Fendant is very successful and a key figure of Valais.

It is a dry, floral, light, refreshing wine and is considered the best to accompany cheese dishes, such as fondue or raclette.

Its alcohol content is usually between about 11 and 12.5% and can be found also slightly sparkling.

The Fendant sauce described in this novel is the fruit of the author's imagination.

DESCRIPTION OF THE PENTALOGY

Book 1: Chef Daniel, *The mystery of the Fendant sauce*

Book 2: Chef Jake, *The Vegetables' Waltz*

Book 3: Chef Michael, *Coralie, my love!*

Book 4: Chef Rick, *To be a Chef, or not to be a Chef*

Book 5: Chef Florian, *A willing victim*

MAIN CHARACTERS

Daniel, Michelin-Starred chef from Cambridgeshire, owner of The Yucca restaurant in London.

Jake, Michelin-Starred chef from Berkshire, runs five restaurants called Jake's in London, Oxford, Carlisle, York and Liverpool, also hosts a cooking show on national television.

Michael, Michelin-Starred chef at the renowned Saillon Manoir restaurant in London, former owner of Le Coralie in Hampstead Heath.

Rick, Welsh Michelin-Starred Chef, owner of the Fully Arvine restaurant in Burton, Wiltshire.

Florian, Scottish Michelin-Starred chef, owner of L'Antre de Farinet restaurant in Glasgow.

CHARACTERS BY APPEARANCE

Lilly, Daniel's lover

Gaston, Head Chef at The Yucca

Benedict, Head Chef of vegetarian cuisine at The Yucca

Boris, Administrator and Accountant of The Yucca

Damian, Rick's brother, Manager of a health centre in Stourpaine, Dorset County

Mr Tornado, Culinary critic, awards the third Michelin stars

Viviane, Junior Chef at The Yucca

Marine, Daniel's former girlfriend

Johana, Florian's wife

Toby, Chef, Daniel's ex-kitchen helper

Marcel, Chef, Daniel's ex-kitchen helper

Jules, Journalist

Euan, Junior Chef

Robert, Junior Chef at The Yucca

Dr Lloyd, Daniel's GP

Hugh, Michelin-Starred Chef, Rick's friend in Wales

Faith, Daniel's housekeeper

Maxwell, Bodybuilder, Daniel's next-door neighbour

Oliver, Junior Chef, Faith's son

Elliot, Junior Chef at The Yucca

CHAPTER 1

Light drizzle licks my face in the darkness of the night, my footsteps resonate on the damp asphalt, the city is peacefully asleep. In spite of the biting cold I take my time appreciating this moment of solitude, too rare, unconstrained, immersed in my thoughts. From the taxi rank I walk the empty streets towards the large and luxurious apartment, where I live alone.

My name is Daniel. "The great starred Chef Daniel" some will say with admiration or flattery; "the horrible and unbearable Chef Daniel" others will say grimacing. My restaurant, "The Yucca", 2 Michelin stars, is one of the most popular in the capital.

For as long as I can remember, I only had one idea in mind, almost an obsession: cooking. With nostalgia, I remember the afternoons spent with my late grandmother who taught me everything. In her house, a family farm in the middle of the British countryside, she passed on to me not only her knowledge but also her boundless passion for food and cooking. Her life was spent with her pots, pans, white flour streaking her cheeks, trying new recipes, experimenting, always innovating, reaching perfection and sometimes inventing as well. She had not had the opportunity to make a living from her passion. Financially, studies had been out of the question. Since childhood, she had known that her only possible future was working on the family farm. When she reached retirement age, she never left the kitchen, devoting herself to her large family, sometimes excessively so. She would taste and re-taste the food, then, hand on hip, she would wait for our verdict, staring us straight in the eyes. It was with a slightly shaky hand that I put my fork in my mouth, as I was a little boy, and in an unsure voice give my opinion. She was only satisfied when the plates were empty on the dining table and her guests declared they were delighted.

It never crossed my mind not to be a chef. Today, cooking is my reason for living.

And there is the money to be made, which obviously does make your life better. When you earn a good living, worries are alleviated. We forget about pain when we drown in work and do not think about what is missing in our lives. My parents' and grandparents' lives were quite difficult, money was scarce in those days. Maybe that is why I wanted to make a lot of money, quickly, so that I would not have to count, I would not have to worry about the end of the month's dreaded bills. For several years now I have earned what some might consider an immoderate amount of money, but yet I am always afraid of not having enough.

Not so bad for the country boy who did not really have the cards in his hand to succeed in life. When I was young, I was abused by other kids. I was the son of a farmer, too poor, too fat, too short-sighted, too badly dressed. Not really knowing how to communicate, I was terrified of speaking in a classroom in front of the other children. I was the butt of all their jokes, a laughing stock. No classmate would dare to defend me, I had no friends. I was given the worst nicknames, the most hurtful ones. I suffered bullying by kids who did not know how lucky they were to have a less hard life than mine. They were just having fun making my school life a living hell.

Then, with the success of my work, things started to change. Today, I regularly appear on national television and the country's main newspapers have written flattering articles about my restaurant. Some of my childhood tormentors got in touch with me, with a mischievous smile on their lips. I sent them to Coventry with obvious pleasure.

Not only have I become one of the best starred chefs in the UK, but I want to be number one. Getting the third Michelin star is only a matter of time. I have no doubt that I will get it. My ambition is all-consuming.

In the icy night, a thought crosses my mind, I could call Lilly, spend some fun time with her and ask her to leave at first light. Lilly, a tall, sculptural, short-haired blonde, has been my lover for a few weeks. A top executive in a bank in the City, very ambitious, I do not think she loves me and I do not care, because I do not love her either. I am often invited to the most glamorous VIP parties. I take her with me, with a rare smile on my face. Lilly is beautiful, her presence flatters my ego.

Before Lilly there was Aline, Jocelyne, Ursula, Caroline, Jennifer, and... I do not really remember the others. The list of my conquests is long. I am not a gentleman; it does not even cross my mind to be one and I do not give a damn about etiquette. When I notice that one of my lovers starts to get a little too attached, I immediately put an end to our relationship. I do not want to be "chained". Then I quickly move on to a new affair.

But tonight, as I slip the key into the lock of the front door of my apartment, I notice that I am quite tired, which does not happen very often, so I decide not to call Lilly. In a few hours I will be again in the kitchen of my restaurant. I am a workaholic. Luckily, I do not need much sleep to get myself up and running. It is not uncommon for me to get up around 4:00 in the morning after having worked past midnight.

At the same time as Daniel prepares to go to bed, in a flat in South London, four friends look sad and terribly worried. Their names are: Rick, Gaston, Benedict and Boris. They regularly meet to talk about the particular situation that bothers them.

Gaston clears his throat and breaks the silence: "I cannot take it anymore. We cannot keep beating around the bush, we have to act, even if it means causing damage and upset. I have come up with a plan".

Then, trying to ignore the increasingly incredulous looks on the faces of his friends, Gaston outlines his plan to them.

When he stops talking, a long silence settles in.

Then, his friends can no longer contain themselves and call him a raving lunatic.

CHAPTER 2

It is Sunday evening. I am in the company of my starred chefs' friends: the Englishman Jake, Rick the Welshman, Florian the Scotsman and Michael the Londoner. We regularly meet at Jake's private home in Berkshire County.

We all worked together at different times in the past. As kitchen helpers, then junior chefs, we sweated and suffered under the orders of the veteran starred chefs who trained us, with much bickering and humiliation, sometimes even beatings. We had a hard time holding back our tears, being mistreated by these old chefs who allowed themselves the worst. This created a bond of solidarity that still exists today, which is why I always take great pleasure in seeing my youthful companions, even if we do not talk much about the past. I guess it is still a little too painful for us.

These difficult years finally paid off. We had the rage to succeed and developed very strong characters. Failure was not on the agenda. Full of pride, we became the elite of British cuisine. Today each of us is recognised, respected, and is the owner of at least one starred restaurant whose reputation extends far beyond the UK.

Tonight, our meeting's aim is to prepare Jake's next TV programme. Our friend hosts a cooking show on national television. As usual, the discussions are lively. Only Rick seems a little quiet. Usually, he is cheerful and makes me laugh out loud with his sense of humour.

Looking at my friends, I allow myself a moment of nostalgia while following the discussion with a slightly distracted ear.

Jake and I met many years ago at the "Lemon Tree". It was one of the best restaurants in London, now dethroned by our own establishments. Already as a young lad he had a strong personality. In terms of glibness, no one can match Jake. If he has an idea in mind, an idea to get across, I challenge anyone to resist him. His imposing physique, his sometimes-overwhelming personality, does not meet with unanimous approval, but goes down very well with the viewers of the television channel that hired him. The public loves good-looking people and Jake, with his pleasant air, his laughing eyes, his sensual mouth, his perfectly groomed ash blond hair, is a star. But one must not forget that behind this carefully maintained image, there is a formidable businessman.

I have to admit that I am a little jealous, despite my sincere attachment to him. Personally, I feel more comfortable locked up in my kitchen with my pots and pans than with my fellow human beings. Physically, I am shorter than him and a bit overweight, although I am careful not to exceed a certain weight, but it remains a struggle. When I look at myself in the mirror, the verdict is final. I am much less attractive than Jake with my straight hair, turned salt and pepper very early on, and my short-sighted eyes. Whatever I do my face conveys a certain sadness. I am not sure why, the seriousness of the work I suppose or a life of hard work. A childhood more often unhappy than happy has left its marks maybe.

On television Jake is great in his live shows, he is never caught off guard by the sometimes-stupid remarks of some of his guests who know nothing about cooking. He plays with the camera; he seduces it like a great actor. No doubt many women fantasize about him. His velvety voice would calm down a furious lioness. While others are filmed with their mouths wide open, sometimes drooling over a piece of food they are tasting, Jake is always perfect even when he eats in front of the cameras, which is a far from easy exercise when you know that millions of people are watching you.

He knows perfectly well how to tame his inner demons, his anger, his moods, at least in front of an audience. In private Jake can explode violently, but no camera will ever witness this. His reputation is paramount in his eyes.

I have often wondered whether this need for recognition, to be constantly in the limelight, does not hide in Jake a more intimate need, a deep wound from his childhood. While Jake often talks about his mother and his brother, I have never heard him mention his father. Instinctively I feel it is better not to approach the subject.

I am proud to count him in my close guard, although sometimes I would like to see him make a mistake live on TV, breaking that all too perfect image of a good-looking guy whose life flows over him, impervious to difficulties. But I know that will not happen. I wish I were like him, but I am not. We are too different. Nature has not spoiled me. He is the lucky one.

We, his friends, are regularly invited to his cooking shows and are more than happy to participate. Let's face it, this is very good for our image and attracts customers to our own restaurants. In such a competitive environment where a reputation can be destroyed in a snap of the fingers any publicity is good to take. And the next ambitious generation is already on our heels. Many chefs dream of being in our shoes. But when we cook live, there is no room for mistakes, hence the rigorous preparation.

After this wonderful evening at Jake's, I am driving home in my luxury car. Tomorrow is theoretically a day off, but I am going to do some paperwork and rethink the week's menus.

Next morning, Rick drives down on the motorway to his brother Damian who lives in Stourpaine, Dorset County. Gaston, Benedict and Boris are already there. They need to discuss the problem troubling them for months. Rick feels anxious recalling the previous evening at Jake's house. With what he has seen, he is not at all reassured. Is Gaston's completely crazy plan the solution?

When he arrives at Damian's house, his friends look at his sinister face with a shiver of horror. In a split second they all understand that the situation has deteriorated even more.

CHAPTER 3

Monday morning, I feel tense driving to work, the roads are slippery, it snowed again last night.

When I bought "The Yucca" a few years ago, its star was not really shining in the firmament after a rather glorious past. To be honest nobody wanted it, but its price was within my limited budget. I invested a lot of money in my restaurant, in fact my meagre savings went into it in a split second. I went into the red until I could not sleep a wink. Over the years, I managed to pay off my debts. Lately, I have been making more money than I thought possible.

I won two Michelin stars. I am working hard to keep them and earn the third. The Michelin guide, which sells like hotcakes, is so influential that the awarding of a star brings a significant increase in clientele. On the other hand, the loss of one is highly publicised, penalising and humiliating. Losing a star would be unbearable. The Yucca is my pride and joy, my life's work.

In order to win this damn third star I cannot make a mistake. Every day the dishes presented to the clientele have to be perfect in case there is a food critic in the room. For some years now the rumour is that the awarding of the third star is in the hands of only one person. It seems to be a man of about 35 years of age. He is said to have nicknamed himself: "Mr Tornado". After his visit, either the establishment has survived, or it is in tatters. Every day, I scrutinize the faces of my guests in order to spot this famous Mr Tornado, without success so far.

The Yucca is located in Brixton, a popular area south of the Thames and the birthplace of pop star David Bowie. For ages it has been home to a plethora of celebrities, including the painter Vincent Van Gogh. There were also some stormy times over the last few decades, to say the least. The area has been the scene of race riots and working-class uprisings in economically difficult times. Confrontations with the police were bloody. Then a relative calm set in and the visit of Nelson Mandela in 1996 marked a turning point. But Brixton's reputation as a brat, a rebel, remained stuck.

Long considered the capital of the Jamaican community in London, Brixton is colourful and full of life. Its music and cultural scene are very varied. Over the years, interesting theatres have opened and offer a programme of classical and contemporary plays. And as the flats in the town centre are madly expensive, middle-class people started to move south, giving the place a new face, more family-oriented. These new arrivals chased away the proletarians traditionally settled in the area, the real estate market forces poverty to move. The inequality of the classes is still active today, or especially nowadays. This evolution has brought in recent years customers with financial means to eat in a starred restaurant.

What also convinced me to buy The Yucca is the fresh products market in Brixton, which I believe to be one of the best in the city. This lively market is a splendour of colours, scents, and vegetables brought directly from the countryside. There is also an incredible variety of fresh meat and fish. A feast for the eyes! The quality is amazing.

My restaurant is located on the edge of Ruskin Park. The proximity of this green area also convinced me at the time that it could prosper. Londoners enjoy walking in parks, the natural corners in the big cities are a luxury. Ruskin Park is no exception to the rule and from the first rays of sunshine it fills up with everything that society can produce in terms of human beings. The park was named after John Ruskin who was probably one of the greatest writers and art critics of the 19th and 20th centuries. Not escaping the reputation of the area, John Ruskin was also very controversial at the time and even today historians are still wondering as to whether this guy was a great man of letters or a foul-mouthed character with a sulphurous reputation, or even a dangerous individual.

The Yucca has a large convivial room and a second smaller one for private banquets ideal for VIPs wishing to spend a quiet evening in total discretion.

With its conservatory, facing the park, an imposing stone fireplace in the main room, diffusing warmth on rainy days, the atmosphere of The Yucca is much appreciated. The restaurant is of course decorated with numerous Yucca trees. These green indoor plants bring a tropical sensation to the place. I make it a point of honour that they are very well cared for. Every week the best gardener in the neighbourhood pampers them. Sometimes my employees say behind my back that I pay more attention to my Yucca trees than I do to my fellow human beings. For once, I entirely agree with them.

Some evenings, VIPs from all over London meet at the swarming Yucca. It is the place to be seen and, on those evenings, I swell with pride. My booking register is so precious that I have a state of the art safe in my office. To have it stolen, as it has happened to some starred chefs, by jokers or jealous chefs, would be a disaster. Anything is possible in my milieu; nothing is spared to harm a competitor.

There is indeed a computer programme connecting the dining room and the kitchen, but apart from that it is true that one day I will have to invest in a more up-to-date and efficient system.

I have surrounded myself with a very competent team that I lead with an iron fist, recruited after many considerations and very hard tests. Being accepted in my kitchen is a real achievement. I only want the best, only the exceptional, only those who stand out from the crowd. I do not want the others, the average, they are unworthy of my restaurant. I throw their application forms away without a glance.

I know that most of my employees fear me, some do not like me at all, even hate me. I do not care. I can replace them with a snap of my fingers. They have no choice but to work with me for the time it takes to build up their curriculum vitae.

My anger and my sarcasm are feared, whoever makes a mistake gets insulted in front of the whole team to set an example. I enjoy the verbal power to crush the employees. And I want them to realise that they should never get in my way in the future if they open their own restaurant. I have worked too hard to get where I am today.

I also value my reputation. When the best junior chefs leave my restaurant after their training, it is good for me and my restaurant, even if my ex-employees no longer speak to me.

My Head Chef, my indispensable right-hand man, Gaston, escapes my anger and wrath. He is good at his job, very good indeed, obedient too. I have no choice but to rely on him. I need Gaston, I know it and he knows it. I had spotted him in a rival establishment, I had literally spied on him. I saw his huge potential the first time we met. It took me a long time to convince him and I had to agree to pay him a very high salary.

Gaston, a handsome man in his thirties, tall, dark hair, has a good relationship with the staff. He favours dialogue over verbal confrontation or humiliation, which I personally do not approve of, but I respect Gaston. He has proven himself to be an amazing chef and that is all that matters to me. For me, a good chef is, what can I say, an excellent chef, a chef who imposes, who is respected in one way or another, whose decisions are not contested, and above all, who is feared. Sometimes, I tell myself that the atmosphere in my kitchen resembles the one in a military barracks, minus the weapons. And I like that.

I have to admit that over the years I cannot stand some guests anymore. I have crossed a few names off my guest list, even though they are important on the London scene. I can afford it; the restaurant is not lacking customers anyway.

Moreover, not knowing when the famous Michelin critic, Mr Tornado, will show up at my place, I prefer to get rid of the cumbersome customers. I do not want those idiots to spoil the Tornado's meal.

I cannot stand the public relations aspect of my job. I find it harder and harder to smile at the end of the evening and listen to those guests who do not know the difference between a lamb and mutton dish and dare to make suggestions. When I am exhausted, I feel like slapping one of them in the face. I can no longer stand their amateurism. Why can they not be content to eat, drink and pay, rather than make their so-called knowledge known, an opinion that I do not give a damn about!

While listening to them, I smile with great difficulty. And if some so-called ladies with plunging necklines and indecent shortness of dress think they have caught my attention with their shrieking voices, I would like to yell at their faces that I find them ugly and stupid, and that I would not undress them for anything in the world. They have certainly caught my attention, but far from the desired meaning! I obviously refrain from saying what I truly think. Afterwards I take my frustration out on my staff. I yell at them.

Then I go home and to relax I listen to booming classical music in my living room, driving the neighbours crazy. On numerus occasions registered letters arrived by post, which I simply ignored, threw them condescendingly into the bin.

Sometimes my neighbours call the police. As if Vivaldi's Four Seasons could harm their sleep! Who do they think they are! I smile at the officers, apologise hypocritically, claiming that with my job I had not realised how late it was.

CHAPTER 4

The team is standing in front of me. I see some of my employees trembling a little, their eyes riveted on the tiled floor. The new kitchen boy who arrived a month ago is so pale that I wonder if he is not going to faint. The final instructions are hammered out for tonight's banquet in honour of the Mayor of London. Once again, I repeat that no mistake will be tolerated and that an exemplary sanction will be applied if a single justified complaint, however small, is made by the guests.

I love those moments of absolute power. Gaston, my Head Chef, remains serene. I suspect he is tired of my anger. But I also know that he will not say a word, he will never contradict me in front of the staff. He is far too intelligent to make this mistake.

Benedict, the chef in charge of the vegetarian dishes, is a man of rather strong build, with a round head and dreamy eyes. During my speech he looks away. I have never managed to shake him, he looks neither angry, nor tired, nor in a good mood, nor in a bad mood, just imperturbable. This chef is a bit of a riddle to me. I sense that my yells have no effect on him and he is not impressed by my bad moods. As a result, tired of seeing nothing but indifference in his eyes, I tend to leave him alone, we do not fight in the same category. He maintains cordial contacts with his colleagues. Only the administrator, Boris, seems to have won his sympathy. I sometimes catch them talking in low voices, I do not know on what subject, they fall silent as soon as I approach.

Viviane is a junior chef who arrived six months ago after having completed her training in excellent establishments, including the "Saillon Manoir" under the orders of my friend Michael. She is a good cook, but I do not like her attitude. When I speak, she looks at me with a touch of irony in her eyes. To me she is a kid who has everything to learn, a microbe, and I suppose that in her eyes I am the annoying old chef, even though I have not yet reached my 45th birthday. She is clearly not too afraid of me. I do not like anyone resisting me, the employees must fear me, not want to rebel, but in Viviane I sense a little wind of revolt in her attitude. I do not want any rebellion, only good little soldiers who work like crazy.

I will have to talk to my administrator, Boris, to find a replacement. I do not want to work with someone who annoys me, it could hinder my creativity. Boris will not be surprised by my decision, he is used to my mood swings, and he wants to keep his job. He will do what I tell him.

Tonight's banquet must be perfect and above all better than at my competitors' where the guests, especially the Mayor of London, are used to dining. I would so much like to have him and his supporters come to my restaurant more often, it would be great for The Yucca's reputation. The slightest misstep tonight will be echoed with filthy slander throughout the city's good society, so the stakes are high. If the work of one of my staff disappoints me, they will be fired on the spot.

※

The evening is coming to an end. The kitchen resounds with the noises of pots, pans and other utensils being cleaned. In spite of my yells and constant pressure, everything went well, the guests were delighted. I was treated to applause when I entered the dining room after dessert. The mayor made a short speech. I love this flattery; I fully deserve it.

The chefs are exhausted after the tension of the last few trying hours. Even Viviane did an excellent job, although I did not spare her; on the contrary I was on her back all evening watching her every move and gnashing my teeth. But she endured, without flinching, the stress of my no doubt unpleasant presence. It is common knowledge in The Yucca that I take it out on her. They all know it, relieved that it is her and not them. Solidarity has its limits.

※

It is 1.00 a.m. The restaurant is closed, the employees have deserted the premises. I should be going home, yet I cannot leave because I am intrigued.

Intrigued, because Gaston has, once again, prepared the "Fendant sauce" this evening. I am surprised that he insists on taking care of it. He should leave this preparation to a junior chef. But his sauce tonight, and for some time now I have noticed, has something extra. It is simply fabulous, exquisite. I have kept a little bit to taste it, curious.

That is what I thought! I am amazed. There is an additional, a secret ingredient that I cannot identify. I taste it again. Incredible!

I am far too proud to ask Gaston what his secret ingredient is. I will have to spy on him next time he prepares it. I do not forget that every chef I train can one day open his restaurant and become a competitor. Gaston is gifted, very gifted. He is a threat. I must find out his secret, at all costs! Especially if the famous Mr Tornado shows up at The Yucca and tastes Gaston's delicious Fendant sauce, it cannot be good for my personal reputation. Just the thought of this happening makes me sweat. Yet this sauce is simple to prepare. We learn its composition and preparation at the beginning of our training. It is mainly made with a very fine Swiss white wine called Fendant, hence its name, balsamic vinegar, salt and a few spices.

Could this be the first sign of Gaston's rebellion? I will have to keep a close eye on him. I taste the sauce again. But what could he have added to give it such a delicious taste? What is the secret ingredient?

Perplexed, I shut the door of the restaurant and go home. I drive my car without respecting the speed limit.

Once at home, in my living room, with a glass of red wine in my hand, I review the events of the evening, Vivaldi booming, to the great displeasure of my neighbours who are banging on the walls. I do not give a damn. They can go to hell!

I need to take my mind off things, to release tension. I pick up my phone and call Lilly, my current lover.

CHAPTER 5

Early morning, Lilly leaves my flat. It is a relief; I was getting tired of her blah blah blah blah. Talking so much at breakfast is unbearable. I like to eat in silence, a religious silence, which Lilly seems unable to understand despite my protests. I will probably have to find a new distraction; she is starting to seriously get on my nerves and there is no shortage of offers. I have a lot of opportunities to meet women. Yet some of them have resisted me, I do not really know why. It annoyed me for a while, then I forgot about it and moved on.

And then there was Marine.

My heart tightens every time I think of her. Why does she always come to my mind when I least expect it? No one would believe that the unbearable Chef Daniel fell madly in love in the past. So much in love that I forgot who I was. I lived only for her; I was on a cloud of happiness. I thought it was going to last a lifetime.

A fatal mistake that I have not made since.

We met when I was working with my friend Florian at a top restaurant in London. We were very young. I was immediately attracted to her. She had something that others did not have, joie de vivre, independence, sometimes she became a bit wild. She drove me crazy. I wanted to have her by my side all the time. We dated for a few months, it was total happiness, at least I thought so. Then she ended our relationship, abruptly, without explanation. She quit her job without notice, not giving me the opportunity to win her back. I was devastated.

Only Florian was aware of the difficulty of the break up. I suffered like a wounded beast, unable to put one foot in front of the other. My friend helped me, accompanied me, yelled at me, pushed me until I reacted. Then work took over, and I started to date women, a lot, I survived as best I could.

As I regularly come across Florian at Jake's, sometimes I innocently ask him, or at least I think I do, for news of Marine. I do not think he is fooled, despite the years that have passed, but he never lets anything show. Florian's wife, Johana, is a friend of Marine, so he is a valuable source of information. Perhaps it is the fact that I still do not understand why she broke up with me that prevents me from turning the page, or maybe it is more difficult to conceive, I let the love of my life slip away. It tortures me, yet I cannot help asking Florian about her. Each time the answer hurts, but I start over again tirelessly. Like a masochist who likes to make himself suffer. I know that she is happy without me. I want to yell, but I cannot. Will the pain, although lessened, ever go away?

I only meet Marine very rarely, she lives in the countryside, in Devon, and works in a local restaurant. She is a very good chef and could easily get a job in a starred restaurant in London, but no, she prefers the country air. Too bad, I would run into her more often if she worked in the capital.

A few weeks after the break up with Marine, Florian left the restaurant, which was a bit more unsettling. At the time, I was mad with pain and drowned in work. I started to take my frustrations out on my subordinates. The pleasure I had in shouting orders, yelling at the weakest, brought comfort in my wound. So, I continued. I became addicted to this unhealthy pleasure.

Being promoted Head Chef of the starred restaurant, where I worked, run by an excellent but ageing chef who lacked character and did not like conflicts, my moods altered for the worse. The boss let me take his kitchen as hostage for my pain. He preferred to play Bridge with his friends than spend time with his staff.

I had especially taken a dislike to two young kitchen helpers, a blond one with curly hair like an Alpine shepherd and a corpulent man with red cheeks. I believe the first one was called Toby and the other Marcel. I yelled at them whenever the opportunity arose. I wanted to break them, to shatter them, to grind them like wheat.

It was perfectly unfair, but it gave me obvious pleasure. That is when I understood that I liked sadism, that I liked to hurt.

And I never stopped.

CHAPTER 6

Although the sun is shining this morning and it is a beautiful day, I am in a killing mood. I am running late and I hate it.

I have an appointment at Jake's TV studio to record his cooking show. I dressed in what I call my "cool" uniform; blue jeans and pastel yellow jumper.

When I arrive at the studio, I meet Jake's team of assistants, beautiful women, my friend is a connoisseur. Comfortably seated in the make-up room, in the expert hands of these sweet young women, who give me a new look, I try to relax. Looking at the mirror I make an effort to show a nice face, to become the gentle chef, a little shy, with a touch of nostalgia in his eyes.

During Jake's show we cook together, in harmony, joking, relaxed. I feel at ease and I can even laugh heartily. We have known each other for so long! And above all, we have fun, despite the rigour and tension. I think it is the adrenalin of live broadcasting that does it.

I am the king of pan-fried foie gras. I developed a successful recipe a long time ago and never entirely reveal it, especially in front of the television cameras. I prepare the mix of spices in my kitchen in The Yucca and bring it with me in a closed container. Even Jake does not know all the ingredients, yet he often teases me about it. My recipe has greatly contributed to my reputation, I probably owe it a Michelin star.

The show goes very quickly and soon enough we have to say goodbye to the viewers. When the cameras have switched off, I wipe my sweaty forehead. Everything went well, perfectly, apart from an incident a few minutes ago.

Among the guests was a young, fashionable, ambitious, beautiful, elegant, arrogant actress, who never stopped flirting, crossing and uncrossing her legs when the camera was not on her, staring at me with a look full of sexy promises. If only she knew how much I cannot stand this kind of behaviour, it makes no impression on me! If I want to flirt, I decide who to hit on.

At the end of the show, she asked for my private phone number, which I refused to give. She was furious that I declined to see her again, to obey her, and made it loudly known in front of the bewildered staff before leaving by slamming the door. Her oversized ego was shocked by my refusal. I have no doubt that she will soon recover.

As usual, the show reached very high ratings. While the technicians take care of their equipment, Jake and I drink a glass of wine. Although I am a little – well a lot to be honest - jealous of him, I enjoy these special moments alone with him. He is the only one who can get me to talk, I confide in him about my inner doubts, my problems at work and my private life. He listens without interrupting. Jake understands me, like me he comes from a modest background and had to struggle to get to the top. I know that nothing I entrust to him will be revealed. And I return the favour.

Jake is always surrounded by friends, acquaintances or family. But I know from experience that you can be surrounded and feel terribly lonely. Jake does not show anything of what he feels deep down inside. He always has an air of detachment and serenity on his face. But is he really happy? Sometimes when it is just the two of us, he lets go, he drops the mask, like right now, and I can see sadness in his brown eyes. Maybe I am wrong. Jake cannot be unhappy; life seems to slide over him so easily. In comparison mine looks like a continuous battlefield.

After the show, I return to the restaurant. I am not the nice guy anymore and become again unbearable. My legendary bad mood comes back when I see two junior chefs chatting quietly in the kitchen while the work is not finished. I explode violently.

I am back to being myself again.

CHAPTER 7

On this beautiful, but icy, winter morning, as I walk past the Brixton newsstand on my way to the market, I see that London's daily newspaper has devoted its front page to The Yucca. I hurriedly buy several copies. As I read the article, I redden with pleasure. I know that I fully deserve this praise. My staff should understand how lucky they are to work with me. I am not sure that these ungrateful microbes really realise this.

The lines are written by the well-known journalist Jules, who regularly dines at The Yucca. He is a host that I cherish and find very interesting. Although I am used to compliments, I did not expect such an honour. The article is great, I feel like framing it. I am going to be in a good mood all day.

But there is a sentence that worries me. Jules mentions the Fendant sauce, calling it exceptional. He does not know that Gaston has cooked it. This upsets me deeply. I cannot waste more time, I must, at all costs, unravel the secret of Gaston's preparation.

One o'clock in the morning, the staff have left, exhausted. I am alone in the kitchen and contemplate the saucepan in front of me. I dip the spoon in the sauce, bring it to my mouth, close my eyes to concentrate.

What the dickens is going on ??????!!!!!!!!!!!!????

But what on earth does he add to his damn Fendant sauce? Once again, it is exceptional, with that little something, that extra flavour, delicious, sexy, that I cannot identify.

This evening some important guests praised the sauce and I had to admit that it was Gaston's. An embarrassment, a shame! But I smiled as I spoke to the guests while admitting the fact that it was my Head Chef who cooked this delicious sauce. Inside, I was bubbling with rage.

I feel that a crisis situation is developing and that I must react quickly and intelligently. Customers have to keep believing that I am one of the best chefs in the country, who regularly appears on TV, and above all that I am THE CHEF of The Yucca, who prepares the best dishes AND the best sauces. I cannot tolerate that my Head Chef cooks better than me. He cannot overshadow me.

I go home angry. It is going to be a short night.

The night was indeed short, I did not sleep a wink. In front of a steaming cup of coffee and breakfast, I decide to take action. In order to unravel the mystery of the Fendant sauce, I look for, and find, a bogus pretext to slip out of the restaurant until the evening. I call Gaston to inform him that I will be away until around 5 p.m., without, of course, saying a word about my true intentions.

I am going to visit my friend Rick in Burton, a small village in the beautiful county of Wiltshire. But today I do not think it will be the beauty of the scenery that will catch my attention. I am so angry that I see nothing but my goal: to unravel this mystery that is seriously starting to spoil my life. Desperate times call for desperate measures.

Rick is younger than me, but I respect him greatly. He started his career at a very young age and won his first Michelin star at 26. We worked together a few years ago when Rick was in London. He is a lively and charming man, easily using his sense of humour to get out of the most awkward situations. He is Welsh, like Gaston. I suspect that there is a special ingredient used in Wales to prepare the Fendant sauce.

At high speed on the motorway, I start to relax. I am happy to act, inaction does not suit me. Rick's restaurant is located in a region that managed to remain rural and unspoiled, far from the major urban centres. Several counties can be crossed on foot along the famous and very popular Cotswold way, which is almost 125 miles long. This bucolic trail goes close to historic sites such as the Broadway Tower and Hailes Abbey, very popular destinations.

Booming classical music in my car, I finally arrive at Rick's restaurant.

My friend greets me with a smile, but looks a little surprised. I find him in a corner of his majestic kitchen, experimenting with new dishes, the daily life of any ambitious and passionate chef. I do not give him any reason for my visit, just that I was "passing by".

After a few moments of mundane conversation, I ask him nonchalantly, looking as detached as possible, the question bothering me: "Hey Rick, do you have your own way of preparing the Fendant sauce in Wales?".

If Rick suspects that this is really the subject of my visit, he does not let it show. Frankly, he probably has other things on his mind.

"Yes, there is indeed an old recipe. I believe I have got it in my office. Wait a second, I will go and get it".

When my friend returns, I quickly pocket the paper he hands out without looking at it. Then we sit down around a magnificent solid wood table, and enjoy a hearty meal, during which we exchange a few confidences and laughable anecdotes about our lives. I find myself relaxed and enjoying the moment. I do not feel like going back to London, I missed the country air more than I thought I would.

However, after a few hours we both have to get back to work. Therefore, I take my leave.

I jump in my car light-heartedly. I vaguely wonder if Rick found my visit intriguing. I actually had nothing to do in the area and no excuse in my busy schedule to waste time and get away from my restaurant. I hope he does not say a word to Gaston. If he does, Gaston will not be fooled. I am sure he has noticed my curious glances in his direction when he is preparing the famous sauce. He knows me as well as I know him.

But for the moment I am in too good a mood to let myself be overwhelmed by negative thoughts. The mystery recipe is in my pocket and it is priceless. I feel superhuman and untouchable. I burst out laughing alone in my car, imagining the look on my Head Chef's face when he realises that I have discovered his secret.

※

Daniel is obviously far from suspecting that, as soon as he leaves, Rick calls his friend Gaston to talk about this visit which has by no means gone unnoticed.

"You will never guess who just dropped by! Your boss Daniel who asked me, hold on, the Welsh recipe of the Fendant sauce. I almost collapsed laughing and had to leave the room for a few moments. I went to the office and photocopied something phony from one of my zany books: Cooking for dummies".

"Rick, I cannot believe it! That is quite a turning-point, he reached a new level of vileness. He called me this morning to tell me he wanted to visit a new supplier. Thanks for the heads up!".

Switching off the phone, Gaston has a smile on his face. Finally, Daniel took the bait. His plan is starting to work. His mystery preparation of the Fendant sauce is driving Daniel crazy, exactly what Gaston expected.

All excited Gaston goes to Boris's office, where Benedict is present. He informs them of the new development. He struggles to read their faces. Are they happy that the plan is working or are they afraid?

Boris answers Gaston's silent question by saying he is terrified.

Gaston reassures them, everything will be ok as long as everyone sticks to his plan.

He does not add that before he can go on with his plan, he has to deal with what he calls "the other problem". He sighs, this is not going to be a piece of cake.

Having spoken to Gaston, Rick then dials the number of his brother Damian who runs a health centre in Stourpaine, Dorset County. A while ago, the two brothers made a bet: which of the starred chefs between Daniel, Jake and Michael will first suffer from a collapse and need a cure. Florian is much more stable and less stressed, like Rick he works away from London and escapes the madness of the capital. Unfortunately, in the last few months it has become clear that the first candidate for the break-down will be Daniel.

"Hi brother, the pressure cooker is ready to explode! You can soon book a room for Daniel and an appointment with the doctor".

The two brothers burst out laughing nervously.

"Little brother, I hope you're taking care of yourself". *Damian's voice could not be more concerned.*

"Do not worry, every time we meet at Jake's place, I tell myself at least ten times: never become like them! They are throwing their lives away, stressed out like madmen chasing after those Michelin stars. I try to tell them to slow down, but their damn pride means they do not get the message. Unfortunately, as we suspected, Daniel is reaching breaking point. He has been pulling on the rope for too many years, even though he has not been aware of it at all".

CHAPTER 8

On the golf course I do not miss a ball. Even if I have not yet tried the Fendant sauce according to the recipe that Rick gave me two days ago, I am sure that Gaston's secret is discovered and I feel lighter, freed of a weight. Lilly has taken refuge at the bar chatting with members of the club, no doubt very wealthy. I suspect she accompanied me just to make contacts with potential clients. Working in a bank requires a constant effort to attract customers. The very short and sexy dress she is wearing today should help her a lot. I do not care if she is being hit on. Here all of London's wealthy people gather on Sundays, rain or shine, it is the place to be seen.

I play golf with Michael and his wife. They have been married for almost two decades, work at the same restaurant, and spend their free time together. How can you spend your days and nights with the same person? I could not stand it; I would become neurasthenic at best. After so many years of marriage they still look lovingly at each other. They share gentle glances, when they think I do not pay attention to them.

Even though he is a well known personality, Michael has managed to protect his personal life. No pictures of the children have ever appeared in the press. The unfortunate so-called journalist, or rather paparazzi, who tries to shatter his family life, is risking a lot. Michael is in friendly and professional contact with some of the most ferocious lawyers in London. They regularly play golf together when they are not on business trips halfway around the world.

Michael had to call on them a few years ago when his business partner ripped him off. It was a very dark story that left a lasting impression on people's minds.

At first, they were friends. They had known each other since childhood and decided to become partners, co-owners of a restaurant on the edge of the park in Hampstead Heath, a rather posh area of London. The restaurant was called "Le Coralie". They invested large sums of money borrowed from banks, especially Michael. His friend was wealthier. The business was going very well, then everything fell apart. Suddenly his partner showed his real face, became authoritarian, wanted to be the sole boss and could not stand the shadow his friend was casting over him. In addition, one day Michael noticed that much of the money he had invested had vanished into thin air. This restaurant, which was supposed to be a dream, the achievement of a lifetime, had become a nightmare. Michael had no choice but to file a complaint and leave Le Coralie with a broken heart. But his ex-friend had become a fierce opponent, with a long and sharp tooth. The legal proceedings lasted months. Michael lost everything, all his money, he was humiliated in public.

He struggled to get back on his feet, working very hard for years. If he regained his financial health, he had lost a lot of confidence. Still today he is deeply wounded, he will probably never completely heal.

While many let him down, laughed at his humiliation, his wife remained by his side, always encouraging and supporting him.

I believe that since this sordid story, Michael cannot trust anyone in business, or in friendship for that matter. Even with me sometimes I am under the impression that he is suspicious, doubtful. Yet far be it for me to want to hurt him, it has never crossed my mind to betray him and I believe that somehow the nightmare he went through terrifies me. It is obvious that my friend is still traumatised, he never talks about it, and if someone dares to mention it, Michael puts him back in his place with harsh words and an icy look in his eyes.

Today, Michael has every reason to be proud, he has become the Chef of the very prestigious "Saillon Manoir" and has been awarded 3 Michelin stars. He rebuilt his ruined career with endless hours of hard work and created extraordinary recipes.

He is the eldest of our small team of friends. I have to admit, and this is difficult for me, that he is better than me. His dishes, which are complicated to prepare, have largely established his reputation as a great starred chef. He is showered with honours and is regularly praised by the critics. Nice revenge!

I worked with him a long time ago and I remember his precious influence, perfection, always and only perfection. It is from him that I get this rigour in the kitchen and this intolerance with poorly prepared dishes. But unlike me, Michael stays polite. He prefers to turn his back on the culprit of a dish he considers a failure, rather than losing his temper like I do.

✻

After our round of golf, we join Lilly at the bar. While Michael's wife makes diplomatic conversation with my lover, with Michael we obviously talk about new recipes to try, our latest experiments, our findings.

We briefly mention with shivers of horror the awful news of the three starred chef from Yorkshire who lost a star following the visit of the critic, the infamous Mr Tornado. This is so distressing that we do not linger on the subject.

I do not think Michael and his wife appreciate Lilly, but being used to my ephemeral conquests they do not make any comments, knowing full well that they will not have to put up with her company for very long. I also suspect that they may have guessed that my break up with Marine has left its mark.

CHAPTER 9

I woke up in good spirits this morning, but it did not last. As soon as I arrived at The Yucca my mood changed for the worse. The junior chef Viviane, instead of being docile and obedient like she should be, stood up to me, which is a big mistake. During the briefing, she contradicted me in front of the whole staff, dared to suggest that she had a better idea for the menu. I saw red and yelled that she should shut up.

Since then, she stares at me and never looks down, which makes me prodigiously angrier.

The tension between us rises even higher during the preparation of the evening meal. The whole team feels it, the other chefs do not dare to open their mouths. I do not let anything pass her by, on the verge of dishonesty. I ask her to start again dishes that I do not think are perfect. I throw them in the bin. I want to break her. She sulks, but she starts her preparations again, tirelessly. Between us it is a duel. I will not be the loser.

Not having really understood the lesson, the next day Viviane's new rebellious attitude is back. Again, she dares to contradict me during the morning briefing in front of all the employees. I tell her to shut up. I am in a killing mood.

I want to fire her. But I do not have time at the moment. All tables are fully booked for the next few months and I have to prepare myself for an upcoming competition featuring top chefs from every county in Britain. The dishes will be judged by culinary journalists.

It took a lot to convince me to take part in this competition, but as Michael, Rick and Florian will attend, I felt trapped. I had to give up and accept with a false smile to represent my region. When I saw that Jake avoided it, I weighed in for a moment. He should explain to me how he manages to say no. I cannot resist the temptation to take on other great starred chefs.

I have to represent Cambridgeshire, my home county. I will have to do some research to stand out from the crowd and find an exceptional dish previously not shown on television.

At the end of the competition, ten chefs will be selected to cook for the Christmas' British Red Cross banquet. In addition, at this banquet, the dishes of the ten selected chefs will be judged and THE best chef in the country will be chosen by the guests. The stakes are therefore immensely high.

I want to be named the best chef in the country; I fully deserve it!

CHAPTER 10

Sunday morning, I did not go to the golf course to meet Michael and his wife. Despite her protests, I hung up the phone on Lilly. Sitting in my kitchen, my cookery books open in front of me, I am working on the recipe for the competition.

As mentioned, I am from Cambridgeshire. At home cooking is not a luxury but a daily act, almost a religion, as my dearest grandmother taught me.

Cambridgeshire is situated north of London, not too far from the sea, where you can fish herring, turbot, sole and cod, which are eaten in a wide variety of recipes. In addition, seafood and shellfish lovers will be in paradise. For carnivores, duck, goose and turkey are raised on rich grounds. Pheasant and partridge are on the menu all autumn long. It is also a region of strawberries, pears, plums and apples in abundance from which delicious cider and juices are made and used for pies, puddings and other delicacies. One can also enjoy some of the best cheeses in the country.

Thinking about the dishes of my childhood lovingly prepared by my beloved grandmother, who passed away too soon, makes my mouth water and brings back nostalgic memories.

My county looks like a typical British postcard. A very green countryside, largely watered by ferocious showers before giving way to magnificent sunshine, lovely villages with their typical church in the middle, elegant manor houses where descendants of old noble families discreetly live, fabulous, beautifully maintained gardens, country lanes where you can stroll for hours on end. In short, a small paradise on earth as far as I am concerned. I always think about my birthplace with a heavy heart. I really do not have enough time to go there anymore. My job is eating up all my life.

And of course, Cambridgeshire has, for hundreds of years, been home to the renowned University of Cambridge. The world's wealthiest families send their offspring there to get an education that is far above average. After the American wave, today it is increasingly made up of Asian nationals. This university is the pride of a whole population, of which I am obviously one.

❅

At the end of the day, my kitchen looks like a battlefield. The effort was worth it, I found the special dish I want to cook. It is a bit complicated, but I know I can master it. There is no doubt in my mind that I will be selected to cook at the end of the year banquet and if with this recipe I am not voted THE best chef in the UK, I might punch a few judges in the face.

My back hurts, seems broken in pieces. I am exhausted. So much for the mess in the kitchen. Tomorrow morning my cleaning lady comes by, she will have a tough job, but she is paid for it.

CHAPTER 11

I am furious, beside myself. But how dare they? How dare they criticise my pan-fried foie gras? It is MY speciality, customers come from far away to taste it.

An elderly countess and her entourage showed up at lunch time. They were not expected. So, we had to quickly find a solution to accommodate them, noblesse obliges. Now they dare to criticize my pan-fried foie gras! It is not to their liking, they whispered with their pinched lips and haughty faces. Benedict, who has the body of a Swiss wrestler, grabs my arm just before I step out to the dining room to tell my way of thinking. Benedict is the only one who can intervene on me this way, with physical force. Usually not very talkative, he pulls me outside through the back door and asks me in an imperious tone to calm down.

He is right, I am out of my mind. My heart is racing, my head spinning. I have to lean against the wall.

I have presented this recipe a few times on Jake's show and was applauded each time. I probably owe it a Michelin star. This countess and her sort can go to hell!

I am so angry that my employees are keeping away from me. Gaston, from the far end of the kitchen, watches me, without saying a word. I believe that today I would be able to throw the pots and pans across the room.

Back home in the middle of the night I am too mad to sleep. Booming Vivaldi music, the neighbours shouting and banging on the walls, I do not give a damn. The doorbell rings, probably the cops, to hell with them!

✳

"Gaston! What is going on?".

"Rick, it is a complete mess! We came very close to a diplomatic incident. Daniel almost yelled at an elderly countess and her entourage. Benedict had to block the way, otherwise he would have gone to the dining room, I believe he could have slapped her!".

"God, I do not believe it, it must be unbearable for you?".

"It is not easy, fortunately Benedict was there and with his imposing physique he pulled Daniel outside, almost had to carry him. It was awful!".

"Well, cheer up old man. I will keep Damian informed. According to his professional opinion, Daniel will soon reach breaking point. Get ready to manage The Yucca on your own!".

"Do not worry as soon as I have managed to solve the other problem, I will have more energy".

"Do not tell me that you have not yet taken care of it? Old man, you are in a lot of trouble!".

CHAPTER 12

The day following the visit of the countess unfolds in great silence. It seems that my employees have lost their tongues. I am waiting for only one thing: the end of the evening. It is time to experiment the recipe of the Fendant sauce provided by Rick.

❈

The crowded restaurant finally emptied out; it is almost 1.00 a.m. I am cooking the Fendant sauce according to the recipe from Wales. Certain of my success I whistle with joy at my victory.

When it is ready, I am very excited. I taste the sauce and in a split second I am disappointed. I taste it again, but I must admit that this preparation has nothing to do with Gaston's unique and delicious one.

The mystery remains complete. A bitter failure! I have to resume my investigation. With an angry gesture I grab the keys of my car and slam the door of The Yucca.

A few hours later, once again sleep eludes me. Usually, I rapidly fall into the arms of Morpheus, but tonight, and this is becoming a habit, I cannot sleep a wink. In my head the recipe of the Fendant sauce goes on and on. What is Gaston's secret ingredient?

In the early morning I get up exhausted with aches and pains all over my body and suffering from a pounding headache.

I am in a foul mood all day long. But I have an idea that starts to relax me deep down inside. Apart from cooking, I have another passion, a recreational one. Religiously, ten days a year I disappear to Sheffield to the professional snooker championship at the Crucible Theatre where the tournament has been held since 1977.

After the visit of the countess and the failure of the recipe provided by Rick, I am in dire need of a change of scenery. The tournament, which starts in a few days, is just what I need. Before he goes home, I inform Gaston that I will be leaving London for a few days. I think I see relief on his face, but I am probably wrong.

Snooker is a discipline that dates back to around the 15th century. It was popular among British officers stationed in India. "Snooker" was the nickname given to a one-year-old recruit in the army. It was used for newcomers to the game and the term has remained ever since. Snooker is played in pairs on a large table of thick slate slabs, which are pressed together. A green sheet is stretched over it. Players must follow a particular and imperative dress code: a suitable shirt, sleeveless waistcoat, dark trousers and neat shoes, not to mention the bow tie, or tie, which is indispensable. Even if the spectators are dressed informally, it would be inconceivable that the players do not respect the dress code in force.

Players must show great manners and fair play, shake hands with each other and with the referee at the start of the match and wish each other good luck.

Basically, snooker is a variation of billiards. Only the cue ball can be hit with a cue (long conical stick) to reach the other balls (15 red and 6 coloured - yellow, green, brown, blue, pink and black). Apart from the red balls that score one point when they are tucked into one of the pockets on the table, the coloured balls score different points, ranging from two to seven, depending on the colour.

The concentration for anticipating the position of the balls after hitting them to always get the best cue ball placement is phenomenal. It takes nerves of steel to play it, the practice of snooker requires self-control and mathematical calculation, not to mention extreme dexterity. The game is complex, it is necessary to use elaborate techniques, practiced a thousand times during training, such as making the cue ball rotate a certain way to modify its natural trajectory and make it come back to the exact point that will allow the player to play the next shot. The most famous players earn millions. They will all be present at this new edition at the Crucible.

I would not miss this event for anything in the world. I have been passionate about snooker since I was a child, tried to play it in my youth, but had to admit that I was not patient and skilful enough.

❈

Lilly was kind enough to come with me to Sheffield. The good atmosphere between us did not last long. We had a huge argument on the second day. She returned to London in tears.

Tonight, is the final match, I am as tense as a bow. Two great champions are playing and I can hardly hide my impatience. Like many, I am fascinated by Ronnie O'Sullivan's game. He can play with both his right and left hands. The audience adores him, unconditionally. Each of his appearances is greeted with great outbursts, like a rock star. One owes it him to have raised snooker to the level of a popular institution and get a lot of young people to practice around a table rather than hanging out in the street.

Ronnie's opponent, with a sad and decomposed face, is suffering total humiliation. The public is overjoyed, conquered and noisily lets it be known to the great displeasure of the judges who are trying to make silence prevail. Ronnie, nicknamed The Rocket, has once again shown that he is a genius.

I would love to welcome him to my restaurant. Unfortunately, he always declines my invitations. However, he did agree to participate in one of Jake's shows. I was terribly upset and jealous that he did. His presence alone had caused the ratings to skyrocket.

After the tournament, I go to the hotel bar and order a double whisky. A few steps away a green-eyed brunette languishes in a sexy dress in front of an almost empty glass of wine. I offer to buy her a new drink. She accepts with a smile.

She will do the trick for tonight.

※

Back in London, Gaston looks at me without saying a word, I seem to detect a certain weariness in his eyes. I must confess that he has done his job properly, the restaurant was very well run during my absence. I am not surprised, but do not congratulate them, it would give too much importance to my employees.

I cannot dwell on that, famous actors are coming to dinner tonight. They booked the VIP lounge in order not to be disturbed. One of them is a vegetarian. I summon Benedict to hear his suggestions. He is an expert in vegetarian cuisine, for a reason that escapes me completely. He is the heir of a long line of butchers. I guess he ended up rebelling.

CHAPTER 13

Before the evening service, I check the booking register. I am not disappointed when I read two of the names written on it. Tonight, The Yucca will welcome the journalists, Jules and Chris. Jules is handsome with a natural elegance, calm and serene, giving the impression of being in a good mood all the time. He and I could not be more different. Chris is a sports journalist. I give the order to place them in the centre of the room, in full view of all the guests. A bit of publicity never hurts and these two are well known. Not only are they famous for their articles in the press, but they also appear regularly on national television.

When they arrive, I welcome them with open arms, as if we were old friends, which we are not. Physically they form an amazing duo, to say the least. Jules is elegant, slender, Chris quite the opposite. He looks like a character out of a Harry Potter book, all flesh and blood, but with a far above average intelligence and an unstoppable sense of humour. The contrast between Chris's job as a sports journalist and his physique, which betrays his personal lack of interest in any form of sport, fascinates me.

They are the two stars of the restaurant; all the customers are glancing at them. No doubt the guests are flattered to be in the same room as these two. Playing the game perfectly, neither of them is fooled that this is good for their careers, Jules and Chris are very accessible, talk to the guests, smile around. I appreciate and admire their repartee, facing these people they do not know at all. With a sigh, I think to myself that I would probably never be endowed with such diplomatic qualities.

Back in the kitchen, I watch from the corner of my eye when Gaston prepares his Fendant sauce. I want to get to the bottom of this mystery. Suddenly, I am distracted by Viviane who asks me a question. This is enough for Gaston to finish preparing his sauce, without me being able to see with which ingredients he completed it.

My anger explodes. I yell at Viviane. But it is too late, the sauce is already on the customers' tables. I am not going to discover tonight the enigma of its preparation. The spying continues and it annoys me deeply.

Gaston looks at me with strange eyes. Has he discovered my haunting for his sauce? No doubt he has.

Back in my flat I pour myself a glass of wine before going to bed hoping that I will sleep tonight. I take advantage of these few moments to take stock and gather my ideas, think about the day and think about what I can improve at The Yucca. Perfection and always perfection to achieve! If I want to get that damn third star, and it is obvious that I want it, I must constantly think about what can be improved.

It suddenly crosses my mind that I am one of the last starred chefs who has not published a cookbook. Michael and Jake have already published a few books. Rick has announced the forthcoming publication of his work and Florian is working on it. I believe the time has come to start writing my first cookbook. I am sure it will be perfect, unique.

And why not include the preparation of the Fendant sauce Gaston's style? I would not be by far the first starred chef to take ownership of a recipe he has not perfected. It is risky, Gaston could get angry and even decide to leave the restaurant. But on the other hand, he owes me a lot professionally. He might even be flattered that I would publish his recipe, without mentioning his name, of course.

Now it is official, I must at all costs unravel his mystery preparation.

CHAPTER 14

Today, almost all the starred chefs in the country are at the London-Bourg Convention Centre situated north of the capital.

The competition to choose which chefs will be cooking at the Christmas' British Red Cross banquet has begun. I am terribly nervous, more than usual, I am not quite sure why, perhaps because I have not slept well again. I curse the day I agreed to take part in this challenge, which is broadcast live on television, but it is too late to retreat. I smile, at least I try, hoping that the cameras do not spot the sweat on my forehead.

A quick look around makes me aware that I do not know all the chefs. I have been long enough in this business, I thought I had met them all. But I notice some unknown faces, very young by the way. The new generation is already here and no doubt they have long and sharp teeth like we did at their age.

The presence of Michael, Rick and Florian does not reassure me - on the contrary, they seem so calm and serene, they even exchange jokes, while I am a bundle of nerves. I take a deep breath and try to reassure myself, of course everything will be fine, there is no doubt, I am the great starred Chef Daniel. But why am I so nervous? I make an effort, despite the tension, to smile when I feel a camera pointing in my direction. Luckily, during Jake's shows I learned to play my part, so this experience will be very useful today.

I must at all costs win my entry ticket to prepare the VIP Christmas banquet. Only 10 chefs will be selected, which is, given the attendance, a small number. The stakes will be very high during this Christmas banquet. I must be recognised as THE best starred chef in the UK. After that Mr Tornado will have no choice but to award me the third star.

The competition started about an hour ago. The sometimes-deafening noise of pots, pans and kitchen utensils clattering together betrays the nervousness of the chefs. Everyone has been assigned a clearly defined and limited space, which makes the work much easier, there is no pushing and shoving, no touching.

I am profusely sweating under my toque, but my movements are precise. In a few minutes my dish will be ready and sent to the judges.

At my side is a chef of about 30 years old, named Bobby. I have met him somewhere but I cannot remember where, probably at a fancy party. From his conversation with his neighbour on the other side I overheard that he is of Swiss and British origins. Ironically, I wonder if he is preparing roestis, a typical Swiss dish. I doubt that the delicate and gourmet palate of the judges will appreciate the unsophisticated side, in my eyes, of this cuisine. But contrary to all expectations, I notice that is preparing a rather fine dish of sole, small vegetables, mashed potatoes and a jelly. He is very calm; his movements are precise. He does not look at anything other than his preparation, nothing seems to disturb him. I suppose it is his Swiss alpine side that makes him so imperturbable. When he has finished and his dish sent to the dining room, I try to strike up a conversation with him. But he does not seem at all interested in talking. He replies coldly without a glance in my direction. Then he starts to clean his utensils and work surface. A Swiss habit, I guess.

His attitude irritates me. He cannot ignore who I am, I am a well-known authority! Who does he think he is, this arrogant young man? What is more, he allows himself to grab his mobile phone and starts a conversation in an incomprehensible language. Swiss-German dialect, I suppose. He acts as if I do not exist. At the end of his conversation, he quietly puts his phone down and ignores me, even though I am only a few steps away.

Very upset by his frankly hostile attitude and not at all used to such lack of attention, I end up raising my voice.

"Do you know who I am?".

He looks straight at me, replies in a very calm voice: "I know perfectly well who you are. Nobody forgets you once one has had the displeasure of crossing your path".

His tone is disdainful and condescending, his gaze icy. I really cannot remember where I have seen him before, it is frustrating. With a sigh, and wanting to forget this little idiot, I look at my friends and notice that Florian has also finished his dish. Without a word for this Bobby, I turn my back on him and join my friend. This young idiot has upset me. Given my seniority and reputation, he should have shown more respect. If one day we cross paths again, I will be very happy to make him pay for his disrespectful attitude.

When all the dishes have been sent to the dining room to be judged, the tension subsides and conversations start to flow all over the place.

After 30 minutes, a heavy silence sets in, we are on the alert for the judges' verdict. The stakes are huge, each of us wants his or her entry ticket to the end of year banquet during which the best chef in the UK will be elected.

※

Suddenly, the head judge enters the kitchen. The chefs hold their breath.

Hurrah!!!!!!!!!! I have got my entry ticket; I am part of the adventure. When my name is spoken out, a huge wave of relief overwhelms me. Then I come to my senses, how could I doubt my abilities? Of course, Michael, Rick and Florian's dishes have also been chosen.

I notice from the corner of my eye that unfortunately Bobby is selected. His less fortunate comrades congratulate him. He smiles broadly, but carefully avoids my gaze. It is a pity; I would have preferred never to see him again.

We, the winners, are warmly applauded by the judges. I love this moment of grace.

Then, with my friends, we decide to have a drink in Michael's restaurant situated nearby. Like an arrogant elite we leave the place. I notice the look of envy on the faces of some chefs who probably would have liked to join us.

Michael did not need much to convince us to celebrate our victory in his prestigious restaurant the "Saillon Manoir", which has one of the best wine cellars in London. My "péché mignon" is a red wine called: Cornalin. This autochthonous grape variety from central Valais (southern Switzerland) has a characteristic purple colour. It originates from the Valle d'Aosta (northern Italy), its presence in Valais can be traced back to the 14th century. It is a complex, spicy wine which goes well with grilled meat, pasta, game or strong cheese. Personally, I enjoy it as an aperitif, preferring a wine with less character to accompany my meals.

Knowing my declared taste for this beverage, Michael hands me a glass of Cornalin that I quickly grasp. We spend the next few hours relaxing and recounting the day's events.

With the relief and the nervous tension gone, I cannot help but share with my friends the attitude of my neighbour in the challenge, Bobby. To my surprise, the others seem to appreciate him and even find him very good.

Given their rather positive reaction I refrain from telling them what I really think of this idiot. What is more, I now recall where I have seen him before. He is one of the two kitchen helpers that I mistreated a few years ago. He was promising, but I was coming out of my break up with Marine and was deeply hurt. I made his life, and the life of his friend Marcel, a living hell. His name is not Bobby, it is Toby.

❈

After the drink at Michael's, back in his car and quite exhausted by the challenge, Rick takes a few moments to reflect on the day and how to sum it up.

Having come to his senses, he grabs his phone and dials Gaston's number.

"Hi Rick, I was worried sick. Boris and Benedict are next to me. Tell us what happened today".

"Hello, I thought Daniel was not going to make it, he was sweating profusely and was terribly nervous. I have never seen him like that. Luckily, he has been selected, like all of us".

"Congratulations for your selection! What you are telling us is worrying. I believe Daniel is on the verge of collapsing. I noticed that he is sometimes mixing up different recipes. That is what happened when the countess was at The Yucca. I suspected he made a huge mistake while preparing the dishes. It was confirmed when I tasted the leftovers he had left in the pans".

"Moreover, I had arranged for him to be next to Toby. I thought he was going to freak out! He was very destabilised by the presence of the half-Swiss. Toby was delighted to play the role of the bad guy and take a little revenge on Daniel".

"Are you mad? Toby? How dare you?!! I would never have taken that risk. That being said, he is trustworthy, I have known him for years. So go home now, relax, and we will keep in touch, thank you, you are a true friend!".

As he turns off his phone, Rick wonders if he really acts as a true friend should. He sincerely likes Daniel and recognises his immense talent. If only he had not crossed the path of the horrible Marine! Everything could have been so different.

With a sigh, he starts his car to go back to his restaurant the Fully Arvine in Wiltshire.

CHAPTER 15

Sunday morning, as usual I am playing golf with Michael and his wife. Once again Lilly takes refuge at the bar to meet potential clients. Although I have not yet discovered Gaston's secret of making the Fendant sauce, I am in a great mood, still happy about the success of the competition.

Then the bomb explodes.

I had noticed that Michael seemed a little preoccupied, a little nervous, ill at ease. Nonchalantly, suddenly, in a slightly detached tone, as if it were a detail, he announces: "I have been contacted by the Shanghai Meridien restaurant in China. They have offered for me to spend a week there in order to present my specialities. Of course, I have accepted the invitation".

I am stunned by this. My legendary jealousy explodes inside me. No doubt Michael was having trouble telling me the news, he knows me too well and feared a nuclear type of explosive reaction.

Unlike me, Michael is often invited abroad, but this time it is different. I am taken aback and find it hard to swallow. I know very well that he is the best of us, probably the best in Great-Britain, but to have his reputation known all the way to China, it is incredible!

In the past, he had presented his dishes in the most prestigious establishments in Europe, in Australia and New Zealand, but never in Asia.

I stammer: "Great, I am happy for you and I think you fully deserve it". I can feel the words hurting my throat as they pass.

Nervousness quickly overwhelms me. I miss my next shots. Then I try to reason with myself, in fact it is only for a week and who knows maybe Michael's sophisticated cuisine will not appeal to Asians. Despite my efforts to put on a brave face, I am terribly upset. I cannot bring myself not to think about it, the news is going round and round in my head. Why did they not think of me instead of Michael? I try to hide my jealousy as best I can, but it is ridiculously difficult.

At the end of the game, I am on the verge of going crazy. I do not stay for a drink as we are accustomed to. On the way back from this disastrous golf game I drop Lilly on the pavement in front of her house, despite her protests, and without a glance I go home in a very bad mood.

Maybe if I listen to very loud Vivaldi music I will calm down. If one neighbour dares to complain, I might hit them.

✳

Monday morning back at the restaurant and still very disturbed by the news Michael told me, I am in a killing mood. My employees felt the wind coming, more like a cyclone, and are keeping away from me. When I notice stains on a tablecloth, I explode violently. The culprit faces me, she is crying. I fire her on the spot.

✳

The next day, Tuesday, I cannot take it anymore. I did not sleep a wink all night. I must do something to calm my frustration, the dismissal of the waitress the day before was not enough to settle my nerves.

I find myself face to face with my administrator, Boris. He is a medium-sized man, impervious to everything around him, constantly looking tired, sometimes a little sad or pensive, I do not know. He always wears grey suits, well cut but too large, his clothes literally float on his skinny body. When he eats, strictly vegan dishes, Boris quibbles with the food. I have often wondered if he is not a bit anorexic. He is not very attractive, speaks little, only when I ask his opinion. Otherwise, he does not say a word, he is a silent person by nature.

Boris does not seem to have any passions or hobbies. He does not talk much with the employees, a little more with Benedict. I have often wondered what those two have to say to each other. I see him arrive on foot at the restaurant every morning, without me knowing exactly where he lives, and he goes to his office where he locks himself in. He spends his day in front of his computer. His domain is accounting, numbers, equations. And in this field Boris is very precious, he is really gifted. Over the years, he has also taken care of the staff redundancies.

My staff management is, let's say, rather peculiar. Boris does not seem to have an ounce of sentimentality. This suits me perfectly. I could not bear to have an employee who lectures me.

I talk to him about Viviane whom I can no longer stand. She keeps talking back to me, which drives me bonkers, and after two sleepless nights, I need to take it out on someone.

"I want you to fire her without compensation. I do not want to see her ugly rat face anymore. I want her to disappear from my sight".

Boris listens to my instructions, which are very succinct, withing uttering a word. Yet I notice something new in his eyes, a kind of reprobation of my decision. Would the dull Boris value someone as voluble and rebellious as Viviane? I find it hard to imagine. However, in a somewhat heavy silence he takes note of my order. Viviane will be notified of her dismissal in the following hour. I will not see her and will not say goodbye. It is her day off, which is why I chose this moment to get rid of her.

I leave Boris feeling relieved to have solved this problem and to have let off steam. I needed to show them who is the boss. The dismissal not only calmed me down but also gave me a good dose of adrenaline. I go to the kitchen yelling orders for the evening. My employees look scared, I like that, no more rebels in the troops. Everything is back to the way it should be. In a mean way, I announce Viviane's dismissal, threatening that it will be the punishment for anyone who does not work according to MY orders. They all stare at me, terrified. I love it!

Boris will quickly place an advertisement in the newspapers to find a new junior chef. There will be no shortage of applications, as usual. And the interviews will resume, once again.

＊

Hidden in a corner of the storeroom, Gaston, leaning against the wall, lets out a long sigh of relief. Phew, at last Daniel has solved "the other problem".

The door opens suddenly. Benedict appears, hands on his hips, looking angry for once: "Are you proud of yourself?".

Gaston does not answer. No, he is not proud of what he has done, but he could not stand Viviane anymore.

CHAPTER 16

I slept very well the night following Viviane's dismissal. As a result, I am having an excellent day at work, even though one less employee is disrupting the organisation.

The "Beauties" have booked a table at The Yucca this evening. These women are extremely wealthy, either wives of millionaires who made a fortune in all sorts of fields, or divorced millionaires who have well-chosen their lawyers. Most of them are famous ex-models. Wherever they go, the media talk about them. They are followed by thousands of internet users. As any publicity is good publicity, I am happy to welcome them. However, they are known and feared when they go out to the city's restaurants, only the most chic and expensive ones. I do not know the reason for this discontent, as I am not interested in the tabloids.

I would soon find out why their presence is feared.

It is the first time they have come to The Yucca and instructions are given to the staff to ensure that they are very well treated. They will be placed at the large table in full view of all the guests.

When they arrive, I cannot resist the temptation to sneak a look from the kitchen door. They are nothing but elegance, designer dresses and rivers of diamonds. I dare not imagine the cost of everything they wear, nor all the money they have paid to their plastic surgeons. The other guests are fascinated by their appearance, nobody dares to say a word.

All eyes are turned in their direction. They seem to be used to so much attention. They are accompanied by their photographer, which fills me with joy. Outside, in front of the entrance of the restaurant, I notice a horde of paparazzi.

Full of pride I go to their table to greet them properly.

❋

In the middle of the evening, I notice a special tension from the Maître D. He seems to be on edge. Although very busy in the kitchen I inquire about his sudden change of mood.

He looks up to the sky: "I have never had to deal with such ill-bred women!".

"What is wrong with you? Get a grip on yourself, my dear, otherwise I will fire you!". I reprimand him severely. He cannot lose his nerve with such wealthy clients.

Hearing unusual outbursts of voices coming from the dining room, I run over there. The scene I face is unreal.

Two of the Beauties are standing in the middle of the room in front of all the astonished guests. These two furies are hurling insult after insult at each other. Their friends encourage them, much to my dismay.

I intervene to stop all this racket and place myself between the two women trying to reason with them. One of them slaps me in the face, the other pulls my hair. I can feel her long nails going into the skin of my head. The crystal glasses shatter, then it is the turn of the dishes to flutter around. These two nutcases grab everything they can, everything within their reach and throw it at each other's heads. Unbelievable!

For the first time in the history of The Yucca, Gaston has to call in the security service. The other customers grab their belongings and run away.

To my horror I realise that the paparazzi outside clinging to the windows have not missed a crumb of the incident.

These women, extremely rich in designer outfits and wearing jewellery worth millions, insulted each other throughout the meal, tearing each other's dresses, disrupting the entire restaurant, scaring the guests, and - icing on the cake - left without paying either for what they consumed or for the damage they caused.

I had never had to face such a situation in my life. Of course, I had to deal with my share of crying spells, divorces, lovers' quarrels, family crises, but never such morons who behaved so shamelessly. One of them even pulled out a lock of my hair when I intervened.

After they left, the restaurant looked like a battlefield. The few remaining customers were stunned. I went to Boris's office to calm down and put disinfectant on my scalp wound.

※

Taking refuge outside, behind the restaurant, Gaston tries to calm down. Sweat beads on his forehead. He is distraught.

Benedict joins him, consternation can be read on his face. He shakes his head and returns to the kitchen without saying a word. There is nothing to say anyway.

Gaston grabs his phone, despite the late hour. He needs to talk to someone.

"Sorry to call you so late Rick, but I am pissed off! We had The Beauties tonight at the restaurant and it was a disaster. Daniel, instead of letting security take care of the fight, thought it wise to intervene. He is suffering from a head injury. More worryingly, he has lost touch with reality, he no longer sees situations as they are and no longer knows how to protect his image. He should have refused to welcome them in the first place".

"Well, another incident that makes us understand that he will soon hit rock bottom!".

"On the other hand, the good news is that he has solved my "other problem"! He fired Viviane. I am super relieved".

"You had better not let him find out how you manipulated him into fixing what you call "the other problem". In the future you will have to learn to get out of your mess on your own".

"I get your point. However, the situation will get even worse in the coming days. You know he does not read the weather forecast page of the newspapers. He is going to have to deal with a situation that might end him. At the moment my plan is working perfectly, he still has no idea how I prepare the Fendant sauce and that, I can see, is driving him nuts".

"I was very sceptical when you told us about your plan in January, but now I am starting to believe in it. Although I still think you put yourself in an impossible situation".

✻

The next day The Yucca is quoted with delight in all the press as the place where the latest Beauties' scandal broke out. The photos taken by the paparazzi leave no doubt. I even appear on the front pages of the celebrity magazines in a picture that creates in me a deep sense of horror and disaster. The photo in question sees me closing my eyes, my glasses crooked, while I try to separate two of the furious ladies, one gives me a good slap and the other pulls my hair!

And, it seems that the videos filmed by the guests are circulating on the internet and are being shared by thousands of people. These plagues have tarnished my hard-earned excellent reputation.

I tell myself, with a sigh, that probably Mr Tornado does not read the tabloids, otherwise I am not going to get my third Michelin star!

My friends call me first thing in the morning to tell me how sorry they are. That puts a little balm on my wound.

✻

A few days later I am appalled to read in the newspapers an article about their "friendship", with a photo on which they pose together smiling.

I will not be caught a second time. From now on, my restaurant is off limits for these indigestible creatures. Money brings neither happiness nor good behaviour.

CHAPTER 17

The heavy rain falling today, Sunday, gives me a very good excuse not to go to the golf course to play with Michael. I am carefully avoiding him since the announcement of his invitation to China, an invitation that transformed me into a green-eyed monster. And I have no desire to see Lilly who is getting on my nerves. Also, given the number of articles about The Beauties' scandal, I want to keep a low profile.

In front of my computer, inspired by a delicious Cornalin at room temperature, I am working on my cookery book. Of course, my recipe for pan-fried foie gras will be revealed. It is my creation, my baby, I want to keep it for myself, not let it go, but I need it to contribute to the success of my book.

After a few hours working, reading the first pages, I am disappointed. The conclusion is undeniable, there is something missing, my writing lacks bite and spice. The whole thing, although harmonious, is a bit bland, like a sauce not tasty enough, a salad without seasoning, a wine with little flavour.

Despite my conviction that my recipe for pan-fried foie gras will be enough, I quickly come to the conclusion that I am missing a recipe out of the ordinary, a recipe that will further establish my reputation.

I am missing a star. It is obvious, I am missing the recipe of Gaston's delicious Fendant sauce! It hits me like a ton of bricks.

In spite of all my efforts, I have not yet managed to unravel this mystery. Gaston must have noticed my stratagem and is now turning his back on me when he prepares it.

Gaston, war is declared! You perfected your recipe in my restaurant, it belongs to me!

I end the day in a slaughtering mood, very frustrated, and with a pounding headache.

CHAPTER 18

After a rainy weekend, the weather did not improve on Monday, on the contrary, the temperature plunged drastically. It was catastrophic on Tuesday with cold showers of rain and snow. This morning, Wednesday, when I open my curtains, I feel distressed.

During the night heavy snow fell on London. Dreadful weather! Never seen before in anyone's memory. As I am not interested in the weather section of the newspapers, it came as a completely nasty surprise.

With a sigh, I quickly get ready to be on time at work.

❋

Taking refuge in the kitchen of The Yucca I try to calm down. The employees arrive late; the bus traffic is interrupted. It is total chaos. I even had to take the Tube, there is no taxi service. In addition to this, from Brixton station to the restaurant I still had to walk for more than half an hour in the snow and freezing cold. I arrived at the restaurant wet and already exhausted.

On top of that, it took us a huge amount of effort to make our way with the van to Brixton market, but once there we were horrified to find out that most of our producers had not been able to reach the capital. As I have always made it a point of honour to cook fresh food, I find myself in a delicate situation, there are simply not enough products in the fridges. It is a crisis situation, a real disaster for lunch and I have got no idea how I am going to manage the dinner. I feel like I am in the middle of a nightmare.

I dearly hope that Mr Tornado does not show up today. I burst into a cold sweat just thinking about it.

※

We cannot serve most of our dishes and have to admit to our guests that we have a problem with our suppliers due to the weather conditions. Unfortunately, our clientele is used to top services. The atmosphere is very tense at the tables. It annoys me tremendously that they do not show more empathy. Once again, my employees have to put up with my very bad mood.

After The Beauties' visit, which has scared away some important customers, here is another day that will not fill the cash drawer. Even Boris looks worried.

※

At the end of this catastrophic day, when the last customers have left, unsatisfied, a very angry Gaston dares to talk to me. He takes a huge risk, given my foul mood.

For the first time he raises his voice: "The situation we endured today is entirely your fault, your organisation is bad and you do not know how to delegate! For at least a week the weather forecast was focused on a snowstorm violently hitting London. You should have foreseen what was going to happen! What the hell were you thinking of?".

I YELL at him in return: "I do not give a shit about the weather forecast, you IDIOT!".

He raises his voice even more, he SHOUTS outright: "You should let me manage this restaurant, the employees would feel much better, you scare them off and do not trust anyone. You are stubborn! The atmosphere is disastrous, which is entirely your fault!".

I do not tolerate his words, his reproaches and yell at him in return: "HOW DO YOU WANT ME TO DELEGATE AND TRUST IDIOTS. YOU ARE ALL INCOMPETENT!".

The situation degenerates quickly, I yell more and more, I cannot control myself. I believe my shouts can be heard all the way to Wimbledon. Like a madman I walk towards him, fists up. I see Benedict approaching and despite my anger, seeing him, whom I know to be ready to intervene with force, makes me stop a yard away from Gaston.

Time seems suspended. Silence settles in. Gaston is staring at me.

Suddenly, he turns around and leaves the room without looking back followed by Benedict who slams the door behind him.

This is the first time I have raised my voice to Gaston, yelling at him. It is the first time he has dared to criticise me in front of the employees and his tone was far from pleasant. He went way out of line, how could he address his mentor, his boss, in such a disrespectful manner? Who does he think he is?

I am too furious to admit that I am especially angry at him for not having succeeded in discovering the mystery of his preparation of the Fendant sauce. With the scene that just happened and all that Gaston had time to tell me before I exploded, I no longer have any scruples. I had none before, but now I want to take credit for his famous sauce for my book, which I am sure will make my success.

"Gaston, calm down! But what were you thinking about yelling like that at Daniel? It is the first time I have seen you lose your temper and I am sorry to tell you, but tonight's scene does not help at all!".

"Benedict, thank you for being there, I thought he was going to hit me. I cannot take it anymore; I am getting seriously exhausted by the situation. Now I must find a strategy to integrate tonight's horrible scene into my plan".

"I really have no idea how you will manage that. Whether you like it or not the situation of The Yucca is looking like the sinking of the Titanic!".

A few hours later, back in my flat, I regret this pathetic scene.

With Viviane's dismissal, one staff member is missing and this is beginning to be felt, we are all tired. Applications have arrived, but too busy, I did not have time to consult them.

What if Gaston decides to leave The Yucca? It would be a real disaster. I have to pull myself together. I cannot apologise to him, I will not go that far, he does not deserve it, but I will make an effort in the next few days. I cannot do without him and above all I must at all costs discover his secret.

CHAPTER 19

Marine is having dinner tonight at The Yucca.

I almost have a heart attack when I see her. I was not told she was coming. I feverishly check the booking register and see that her name does not appear in it.

She came accompanied by an attractive young man. I hate him already. I feel like strangling him, kicking him out. Just knowing that my former love, the one I cannot forget, is only a few steps away drives me crazy. In the kitchen, I cannot concentrate while preparing her order. I am sweating profusely and repeatedly have to wipe my foggy glasses. My hands are shaking.

Gaston smiles in his corner. Since our violent argument we have hardly spoken to each other. Tonight, he seems to be greatly appreciating my discomfiture. He knows very well that I am crazy about Marine. He takes his revenge by watching me, mocking me, without even hiding his enjoyment.

And what was bound to happen, happened.

I completely messed up the preparation of the dish ordered by Marine. Nervousness took over, as soon as I think about her, my brain gets stuck and I can no longer function normally. She sent the plate back to the kitchen. Ashamed of myself, I feel pathetic. The food is a real disaster, the fish is barely cooked, small lumps float on the sauce and the vegetables are a bit burnt. How could I let this happen? I am not about to win her back.

I leave it to Benedict to cook her dish. I no longer trust my abilities. Feeling miserable, I remain confined to the kitchen and have no intention of greeting the guests.

Then I am told that Chef Marine wants to see me, this is communicated by the new waitress who knows nothing about my past. She spoke out loud in front of the kitchen staff. So, I have no choice. With a hesitant step I walk to the dining room. All my employees are holding their breath. Gaston broadly smiles at my defeat.

I find it very difficult to speak, sweating profusely, my heart is running a marathon. Marine smiles, is rather nice. I try to make diplomatic conversation, but all I want to do is run away and take refuge in my sacrosanct kitchen. I only take a quick look at her companion, whom she does not really introduce me to. Personally, I do not want to show him that he matters.

The last few days have been disastrous to say the least. I have always secretly cherished the dream of winning Marine back by impressing her. How could I impress her with all these disasters? She has many contacts in London. I am convinced she was informed about what has gone wrong in The Yucca lately. Some probably would not hesitate to shoot me down - trust me. Everything is known, everything is discussed, everything is criticized, especially the failures and the setbacks. A merciless world.

What is more, I see a ring with a large shiny stone on the fourth finger of her left hand! I am devastated. She is so beautiful; she has not changed at all. I desire her as much as before, no, more than before. It is unbearable.

Back in my flat after that awful evening, I cannot forget Marine. Her eyes, her beautiful hair, her complexion, her smile, her silhouette, her perfume. All these thoughts run in a loop in my head. I cannot sleep.

✳

"Hi Rick, you will never guess who dined at The Yucca tonight?".

"Hi Gaston, tell me more!".

"I will give you a clue. She showed her ugly face accompanied by a handsome idiot. I had not foreseen the move as she did not book under her name, otherwise I would have refused her".

"Marine! I do not believe it! You can count on her to turn the knife in the wound when everything goes wrong. How did Daniel react?".

"As expected, he lost all his senses, a real disaster, completely ruined her dish, which she had great pleasure in sending back to the kitchen. Even if he had succeeded with her dish, she would have sent it back, just to humiliate him".

"One can count on that ratface to belittle people. Well, I can see that the situation is getting worse".

"Sure, it is!".

CHAPTER 20

I had nightmares all night long about Marine, and the Fendant sauce. Seeing her again disturbed me deep inside and not understanding Gaston's preparation of the Fendant sauce drives me crazy! I should call in sick at work, but I cannot. It is recruitment day to replace Viviane.

The young woman sitting in front of us is shaking a little. I frown as I read her reference documents. Since I was not satisfied with the responses to the advertisements posted in the various trade journals, I appealed to my friends. They played along and warmly recommended a chef who worked at their restaurant.

Four candidates who were staring at each other in front of Boris' office when I arrived. The choice is difficult. Benedict and Boris do not say a word. Yet they are supposed to help me. But neither of them seems eager to express his opinion. Probably for fear of seeing me explode like I usually do.

Boris of course takes care of the administrative side and I asked Benedict to attend because even though he does not talk much, I noticed that he has a real flair for people. This is probably due to his highly developed sense of observation. He is rarely mistaken in his opinion of people. I dare not imagine what he thinks of me.

※

Two hours later the interviews are over. We hire Euan, a young chef from Oxford. He has worked with Michael in the past and has come through with honours, which is no small feat.

I inform the successful candidate. He thanks me warmly. He will begin his work at The Yucca tomorrow. We badly need help. I feel relieved to have solved this problem.

※

The relief is short-lived. The next morning Euan does not show up for work. He calls Boris to inform him that he has been offered a better job.

I am furious, out of my mind and yelling at the top of my lungs! What offer could be more interesting than working with me?

Of course, I want to know who stole this excellent cook from me. Who dared to do this to me? I grab my phone and call Euan. He is disconcerted on the phone, but tells me that he was contacted by Chef Toby after our interview and that the latter made him an offer he could not refuse. I slam the phone down.

I am doubly furious. Who does Toby think he is? He snubbed me at the competition in London-Bourg and now he steals my chef! I try to reach him on the phone several times, but his assistant keeps telling me that he is not available. I detect a touch of irony in her voice.

One day Toby will see what I am capable of! I will get even as soon as the opportunity arises.

I tell Boris to contact the candidate who came in second and set up a meeting in the afternoon. I want to interview him again to make sure I only have the best in my restaurant. This candidate, named Robert, was recommended by Rick, which is an excellent reference in itself, but I am offended that Toby stole the candidate presented by Michael, the best chef in London!

At 4.00 p.m. Robert is standing in front of me, his big green eyes seem to be torn between hope and questioning. As I have no more time to lose, I hire him after a short discussion and, to the restaurant's advantage, he was trained in vegetarian cuisine. He will give Benedict a helping hand, because in this culinary speciality The Yucca is a bit behind and I do not like to be behind, especially as the demand for these dishes is increasing. I want my restaurant to be at the top in every aspect, even if I do not understand how one can be satisfied with vegetarian food. When I see a guy, a real guy, order a salad with vegetables, even if it is apparently delicious, I want to yell in his face to put his trousers back on!

"Gaston, you are insane! If he finds out that you called Toby to tell him about Euan, Daniel will bake you in the oven!".

"I know, Boris, I know, but it is part of my plan. I have known Toby for years; he will never utter a word. You know the Swiss have an innate sense of confidentiality; it must come from their banking secrecy".

"Banking secrecy no longer exists and you might soon be six feet under".

CHAPTER 21

"Michael is in China. He left yesterday morning. I took him and his wife to the airport. They were very excited!".

It is Jake on the phone. I was in a good mood, but it is over. I cannot digest the fact that Michael was invited to Shanghai instead of me. However, I make a superhuman effort on the phone to speak in a detached way.

Unaware of my inner turmoil at the other end of the line Jake proposes upon Michael's return to meet at his home to hear about his Asian experience. I have absolutely no desire to listen to pompous Michael, but I agree, not really having a choice.

I rest the handset in a more than slaughtering mood and breathe deeply. It is the first day of Robert, the new recruit. I am going to personally take care of him and take my frustration out on this brat.

※

"WHERE IS GASTON?". I am yelling at the top of my lungs. The employees are on the verge of fainting. I am beside myself. No one answers because no one knows.

Usually, Gaston is always right on time, but not this morning. He is late, two hours late, and is not answering his mobile phone. Already Jake's call had made me more than angry, Gaston's absence is unbearable.

"Benedict, where is Gaston?".

"Not a clue, chef".

Although he remains stony, Benedict, for once, looks at the floor to avoid my gaze. I will not get anything out of him, I know him too well and go back to my pots and pans.

If Daniel had seen Benedict's face, he would have noticed that he was trying to hide his smile.

CHAPTER 22

5.00 a.m., I look like a zombie. Once again, I slept very badly, but this time it was not just the Fendant sauce that kept me up all night. After my outburst with Gaston, I no longer understand anything about him. He has become a complete stranger.

Three days ago, he arrived at the restaurant late, but that was not what upset me the most. He looked, how can I put it, transformed, radiant, as if a light emanated from his whole body. He was wearing large clothes, not at all his usual style. With a huge smile on his face, he told me that he forgave my hurtful words, my outbursts, my bad temper and that he loved me. Then to my utter horror, he took me in his arms for a tight hug and kissed me on the cheeks, two drooling kisses! And this in front of all the employees who were watching the scene with round eyes.

Too surprised and shocked, I could not say a word and just stood there with my arms dangling, not knowing how to react. Having no desire for a second hug, nor drooling kisses, I keep away from Gaston who has been in a light and pleasant mood ever since, impervious to any annoyance.

Even when I start yelling at a kitchen helper, Gaston looks benevolently and smiles, then he gently taps me on the shoulder: "Everything is fine Daniel, relax!".

His attitude either annoys me prodigiously or, exceptionally, calms me down. I do not understand what is going on and I am suspicious, I am convinced that his new attitude is hiding something. I am so intrigued and surprised that I almost forget to spy on him when he prepares the Fendant sauce.

✳

After a few days, I cannot take it anymore and summon Benedict to my office: "Benedict, put me out of my misery, what is going on with Gaston?".

He takes a deep breath and sighs, then announces with a most serious look on his face: "Chef, it is meditation and yoga!".

Apparently, Gaston discovered these practices through a group with Buddhist connotations and is totally involved in this new form of life. I am sceptical, and here I am with a Buddha in my kitchen? That is all I need! At least he has not lost his skills, he even cooks while whistling or singing I do not know what hymn, making all the staff in a good mood. Except me. I am on the verge of freaking out when I hear these weird sounds.

I have absolutely no idea how to handle Gaston's new attitude and as usual when I do not know how to handle a situation I either start yelling or do nothing. My yells have not produced any results, I try to put up with him as best I can. But it is horribly difficult. I do not dare go near him anymore, because I am terribly afraid of his drooling kisses on my cheeks and I cannot stand his fingers tapping on my shoulder when he asks me to calm down.

This new atmosphere in the kitchen makes some of the employees laugh behind my back. However, I cannot help but notice that the food is still as well prepared, or even better, and that is all that matters to me. So, I leave Gaston to his delirium, for the moment. I tell myself that if the famous Mr Tornado eventually comes to eat at The Yucca he will be well taken care of. Moreover, I no longer have the choice of letting go, I suffer daily from a shooting headache.

Every day I expect Gaston to arrive with his head shaved and draped in clothes like a monk.

A week later, completely flummoxed by Gaston's new attitude and needing to confide in someone, I grab the phone and tell Rick everything.

My Welsh friend laughs out loud at the other end of the phone, to my astonishment.

"Daniel, I ought to tell you something about Gaston!".

Then he explains that in the past, in his youth, Gaston had what Rick calls "identity crises". Rick tells me that Gaston shaved his hair, except for a purple crest on the top of his head, for a period of time, then converted to another religion, he can no longer remember which one, then Gaston trained to become a bodybuilder, the list goes on and on.

I listen in amazement to Rick's words and find it very hard to believe what I am hearing. I have been working with

Gaston for a few years now and he has never given me a different image of himself than the one I had before this change. A well-built man, serious, calm, not really having a sense of humour. I could not have been more wrong.

Rick goes on to explain that every time Gaston encounters a big upset, heartbreak or something like that, he has an identity crisis, somehow, he breaks down and radically transforms himself. Like a fuse blowing up in his brain.

He ends with a sentence that makes my hair stand on end: "Do not even think about changing him now, you cannot do anything about it, wait for the next crisis to see what he will turn into!".

So here I am, our big clash probably triggered Gaston's identity crisis. I hang up the phone, more perplexed than ever.

Rick, tears running down his cheeks, grabs his phone and dials his brother's number.

"Damian, you are never going to guess what Gaston has found for his plan, it is so funny, he makes me laugh out loud. Benedict and Boris are in on it! I do not know how they manage to stay serious! Daniel just called. I had all the trouble in the world to act normal, although I was expecting his call. I told a lie as big as a whale and he swallowed it, the idiot!".

Following Gaston's tale of his so-called identity crisis, also laughing, tears running down his cheeks, Damian replies: "Ok, I will book a room for Daniel. He will be here soon!".

Then the two brothers burst out laughing on the phone.

CHAPTER 23

When I receive Jake's phone call inviting me to his house to celebrate Michael's return and hear the story of his culinary adventure in Shanghai, my head is spinning and I have to focus on my friend's words struggling to get into my brain. I had totally forgotten that Michael was in China. My life is in such a turmoil to the point of forgetting my legendary jealousy.

I feel unsettled and I am at a loss. Gaston's identity crisis occupies all my thoughts. I try to deal with daily matters, but I am wading into a new, previously unknown, world. Faced with Gaston's benevolence, who takes more and more initiatives with a huge smile and a communicative good mood, I lose a bit of territory every day. I even forget to yell, part of me feels helpless, part of me wants to fight, but against what? Against the too good mood of Gaston? How can I re-establish my authority with my Head Chef draped like a monk?

Wanting to take my mind off things for an evening, it is of course with pleasure, and a certain relief, that I confirm to Jake my presence in his mansion.

On the evening in question, I could not be happier to escape Gaston.

Once at Jake's place I park my car in front of the entrance of the mansion, the gravel crunches under the tyres. My friends are already there. We greet each other warmly.

As usual, Jake cooks in front of us. We sit around his kitchen-bar on high stools and listen to Michael. His stay went very well, he tasted the most refined culinary specialities, was welcomed like a king and, the icing on the cake, his wife loved this fantastic city (knowing their fusional relationship, this point is of the utmost importance, because if Madam had not liked the place, Michael would not have liked it either....).

The first thing that surprised Michael, and which also surprises us, was that we expected the Shanghai Meridien to be in one of those hyper modern towers, those new buildings typical of metropolises whose restaurants are usually on the top floor. But not at all, the Shanghai Meridien is a building in Gothic architectural style with a pyramid-shaped roof 20 metres high. The restaurant is located on the Bund, a long street on the bank of the Huanpgu River, in a district called Pudong. Michael tells us that there is no underground station connecting the Bund to the centre of the capital, and that Bund in Chinese means "muddy bank", but is called waitan by the locals which means "the bank of foreigners". Indeed, along the Bund is everything that the West has brought to the East, at least in terms of business: French luxury boutiques, international banks, insurance companies, nouvelle cuisine, etc. The Bund is magnificent, a tourist attraction not to be missed, where Michael loved to stroll with his wife. The buildings along it are in Gothic, Renaissance, Baroque and even Art Deco styles.

The way of working in China is very different to the way we work in the UK. The staff impressed Michael with their diligence, knowledge and were very focused on his teaching.

I do believe they did not say a word when Michael was explaining the composition of his dishes. They are difficult to prepare, to say the least, and Michael is not in a playful mood when he is working, which must not have escaped the local chefs. Moreover, he works terribly fast, which is not easy to follow when you hear instructions in a foreign language and with a strong London accent.

While Michael was telling us about his experience, Jake prepared a delicious dish using vegetables from his garden, absolutely great in its simplicity, but no less delicious. We did not leave a crumb of it and swallowed the whole meal accompanied by a Cornalin of a great year.

Then follows the dessert, no less exquisite, the famous "Swiss roll". After we sat down in the sofas in front of the wood fire of the living room Jake opens a bottle of an over-ripe grape wine.

My calmness does not escape my friends. They are not used to this attitude, rather to my nervous breakdowns and sarcasm. With the help of the wine, they finally pop the question. Their curiosity makes me smile.

I take a deep breath and explain to them the transformation of Gaston following our quarrel, a transformation that leaves me more than astonished and somewhat lost, not knowing how to react.

Faced with the bursts of laughter from my companions who cannot hold back, I find myself telling them everything about Gaston; his identity crisis, his drooling kisses on my cheeks, his hugs, his clothes, etc. I find myself totally and theatrically letting go, which gives me a lot of pleasure and relieves my tensions. Of course, Rick adds to this by recounting certain events from Gaston's past, and speculating on what might await me one fine morning when I arrive at The Yucca. We imagine the most amazing situations, to everyone's delight.

My friends laugh so much that some of them have to hold their ribs with tears in their eyes. Michael looks a bit annoyed; I think I stole the show with my story, he does not like not being the centre of attention.

Later when I find myself alone in my car on the road back to London, I reflect that my friends have gone wild tonight, especially Rick. With a more than detached air he made fun of me. But I did not get angry, on the contrary I joked a lot. It was as if Gaston's meditative crisis was beginning to rub off on me, whereas in the past I have always tended to take offence and take the slightest remark or criticism badly. My friend had never dared to speak to me before in such a detached and playful tone, my rather austere air slowed him down on more than one occasion.

Rick is about to unlock his car parked in front of the mansion. Phew, the evening went well! Seeing Florian, who is sleeping at Jake's tonight, approaching, he fears what will happen now.

Florian's face could not be more serious, he is not in a good mood, not at all. He made an effort during the evening to laugh, like the others, but deep inside he felt an anger rising.

"So, Gaston is going mad, just like he has gone crazy in the past! Rick, I have known him for years, I have worked with him, and I have never seen him break down. What is this nonsense?".

Rick swallows a little painfully. Nevertheless, he decides to tell him the truth.

"Listen Florian, Daniel is not doing well. The Yucca is also doing badly. Daniel is too tired to notice it. The customers are keeping away from the restaurant, so Gaston has come up with a plan to try to make Daniel understand that he needs to change. We believe that Daniel will soon hit rock bottom, he has been pulling on the rope for too many years. I am in it because I am trying to help".

Florian's face relaxes. "I know that The Yucca has lost customers. Rumour has it that if Mr Tornado shows up at the restaurant, not only will Daniel never get his third star, but he could lose all his stars. Michael and Jake are completely unaware of Daniel's condition. I understand that you want to help him. If there is anything I can do, please let me know!".

"Actually, there is. We need to keep Daniel away from The Yucca for a week, so that we can set up the next phase of the plan. Could you invite him to Glasgow?".

"With pleasure! I will tell him that he will spend the first evening alone with Johana, as I have to work in the kitchen. He will not resist coming all the way up to Scotland as he is adamant to have information about Marine".

CHAPTER 24

The staff are in turmoil. Nervousness is palpable. I notice that they find excuses, even the most ridiculous ones, to leave their place of work. I do not tolerate this new rebellious attitude and bark the order to stop coming and going and to confine themselves to their place of work.

I wonder which fly has bitten them. Then I consult the booking register and everything becomes clear. How stupid human beings are, men sometimes make fools of themselves!

Katherine Jenkins is having dinner tonight at The Yucca.

I call the Maître D. I am not happy that he did not consider it useful to inform me of the presence of a VIP. But, with red cheeks, he is just as disturbed as the other members of my team. He simply forgot to tell me about it.

Katherine Jenkins is a dazzling beauty. She is a well-known operatic singer. Her voice is rich, delightful and her kindness makes her one of Britain's favourite personalities. She has an angelic face, a porcelain complexion, silky blond hair, big blue eyes and a slender figure.

She is accompanied by her husband, who is just as hot as she is. They are adorable. How can you not love them? No scandal, never in the tabloids, never one word higher than the other. We see them more often at charity events than in restaurants and certainly not in nightclubs.

As they are very strict vegetarians, they tell me that they have specially chosen The Yucca, having recently heard about our new menu. I cannot believe it! If the beautiful Katherine Jenkins eats regularly at the restaurant, it will certainly attract a lot of customers!

As Benedict is in charge of the vegetarian dishes, at the end of the evening I send him to the Jenkins' table to introduce himself. If he, flanked by Robert, the newcomer, comes back to the kitchen unimpressed by this luminous encounter, Robert, red as a lobster, does not manage to say a word for the remainder of the evening.

The beauty of Mrs Jenkins has struck once again.

✳

"My dear cousin, how are you?".

"Hi, we had a great evening, thanks again for the invitation. We need to see each other more often!".

"Yes definitely! But with your busy schedule and my job, it is not easy".

After small talk and thanks, Gaston rests the handset with a sigh.

Gaston and Katherine Jenkins are distant cousins. They have known each other all their lives and as children they used to play together in the sand on the Welsh beaches.

Gaston hopes that his cousin's dinner at The Yucca will come out in the press and that bookings will resume.

CHAPTER 25

After the beautiful Katherine Jenkins' visit to The Yucca my spirits are high. It was very quiet today at the restaurant, only a few guests showed up, which is unusual, but I do not worry about it. Even though I am getting used to Gaston's change, or rather resigned to it, as I do not have a choice, I have not given up the idea of discovering his preparation of the Fendant sauce. On the contrary, I am more determined than ever. The Buddhist Gaston is a little less wary of me. But the fact that I am feeling very tired has taken away what little energy I have left at the end of the day and I have put that idea aside. Until tonight.

I am alone in my kitchen after the employees have left, it is almost midnight. I thought I saw Gaston using Cayenne hazelnut. As I was standing a few yards away from him, I am not so sure. Cayenne hazelnut is not usually used in the preparation of the Fendant sauce. Is this the mystery ingredient?

Intrigued and very excited, I feverishly devote myself to preparing the sauce with this new information in mind.

And it is a failure again. It is not Cayenne hazelnut that I thought Gaston used tonight. The result is irrevocable. It is frankly bad and I throw the sauce in the sink with an angry gesture.

I hate this feeling of failure that invades me every time I think I have got the solution. I am as mad as hell when I slam the door of the restaurant and go home.

❋

Back home, Gaston has a guilty conscience. He wonders what taste the Cayenne hazelnut will bring to the Fendant sauce. He pretended to use it tonight, sensing he was being watched by Daniel.

Cayenne hazelnut with the normal ingredients of the Fendant sauce, the result must be a filthy mixture!

CHAPTER 26

After our morning round of golf, I spend the afternoon with Lilly. Outside it is freezing cold. Spring is having a hard time making its mark this year.

Lilly, usually in such a voluble and energetic mood, is calm for once, which I like, hence my proposal to spend a few hours in my flat, a proposal I am not in the habit of making.

However, with a glass of Cornalin, our conversations are less superficial. So, I learn that Lilly, like me, is from the countryside, that she had to work hard to get her prestigious job. She is aware that she could lose everything depending on whether or not the bank is doing good business. I realise that I do not really know the person who has been sharing my bed for the past few weeks.

She then talks about our relationship, but now she is entering dangerous highly mined territory. I do not like to talk about feelings, and make her understand in a suddenly dry tone not to venture into this kind of discussion. She looks sad, but I do not care.

Not wanting to prolong this unpleasant moment, I ask her in a harsh voice to go home. I do not even give the excuse that I must get up early, I just want to get rid of her and call a taxi. I slam the door behind her. A little annoyed, I turn on the stereo, Vivaldi's notes yell into the loudspeakers.

※

She leaves Daniel's flat in tears. The taxi driver looks at her in his rear-view mirror, then without a word, hands her a box of tissues. She cannot even thank him; her throat is tight. She just nods.

Back in her flat, she calls her brother: "Hi, Daniel misbehaved again. I love him, but I am starting to realise that he does not care about me".

"Little sister, I am sorry to hear this, but are you not getting a little tired of being treated so badly? You will never change him. You deserve much better, you deserve to be happy with a decent guy!".

"Maybe you are right".

"Anyway, he will not see me in his restaurant again! I went there to please you and try to connect with him, but he and I cannot get along. I cannot get through to him and I do not think he has understood that we are brother and sister. I cannot imagine what our father would think if he knew how he treated you".

"Please do not say anything to father! He would not resist the temptation to go to The Yucca and we both know what would happen next".

❋

After our last evening at Jake's, Florian called me to propose spending a few days at his place to improve my Scottish culinary knowledge. His call surprised me, but on reflection would it not be a luxury to get away from London for a few days, and it has been an eternity since I have taken a few days off. On top of that, I am tired and worn out. I am also suffering from daily headaches; it makes my life miserable. The situation with Gaston, and the fact that I do not know how to manage it, is deeply disturbing me. I am in a new environment, certainly Zen, but hostile as far as I am concerned. I do not like it when a situation gets out of hand, and God knows it is at the moment!

Lately, I have also felt something like sadness invading me. I am too proud to pronounce the word "depressed", which I cross out of my vocabulary. So, I ignore it. Sleeping has become difficult. Even when I manage to snooze for a few hours I wake up exhausted. A short stay away from London can only help me get back on my feet.

Not wanting to see Lilly, or talk to her, she had irritated me with questions about our relationship, I take advantage of the opportunity offered by Florian to flee to the North for a few days. Gaston, despite his delirium, has lost nothing of his professionalism. On the contrary, his creativity seems to be exploding in the right direction. During our violent argument, he blamed me for not trusting him enough. Therefore, I decide to leave him entirely in charge of The Yucca for five days.

When I start the car, I am a bit upset that Gaston found my idea "fan-tas-tic". To sum up, he is very happy that I am going away for a few days and told me so with a huge smile and much serenity. He could have hidden his joy! But no, the new Gaston is relentlessly frank. Apparently not saying what one feels deep down inside is not good for something called the aura, or a certain inner balance, or one's self, or whatever! This is what he announced in a thunderous and somewhat messianic voice on a beautiful sunny morning when he arrived at work and wanted to kiss us all. If only he knew what my inner self wants to tell him!

An undisclosed reason for my visit to Florian is also to get some information about Marine. I have not forgotten that during her disastrous visit to The Yucca last month, she was accompanied by a handsome young man and was wearing a ring that might well be an engagement ring. I am anxious to investigate what is going on in her life. Johana, Florian's wife, is a friend of Marine.

"Gaston, you can stop fooling around, Daniel has gone. Stop playing the monk, you are being ridiculous!".

"Boris, I have no choice. The employees do not know that I am playing a role. I must continue to act while the boss is away and believe me, that is not easy. There was even one kitchen helper yesterday who asked me about yoga! I avoided answering him as I have never set foot in a class!".

Benedict has just entered Boris' office.

"What are you two talking about? How much longer is this masquerade going on before I explode, either with laughter or from a nervous breakdown?".

"My dears, I am Gaston the Buddhist! I bet that by the time Daniel gets back from Glasgow I will be able to get him on

his knees. I just need to think about what he might find unbearable upon his return".

Boris and Benedict look at each other helplessly.

They sometimes wonder which one is crazier, Gaston or Daniel?

They also wonder if Gaston's plan will not backfire.

CHAPTER 27

On the motorway having reached my cruising speed, I start to relax. To my eyes the British countryside is the most beautiful in the world. The scenery can change quickly, one must not forget that we are on an island. From bright sunshine, a few miles further on we can find ourselves under the clouds, even under a violent downpour, with changes in the colours of the sky, a particular light which in my opinion only exists at home and magnificent rainbows. I do love my country.

After a few hours of driving, as I approach the first indication of Greater Manchester, my heart tightens, as it always does in this very place. I will never be able to drive through this area, despite the fact that Manchester is beautiful, without having painful memories coming back to mind. As a child I was shocked by the horrific story of the Saddleworth Moor murders that had taken place a few years before and which traumatised the whole country. A couple of psychopaths in the 1960s kidnapped, abused, killed five innocent children and buried their bodies on the moor. I still remember the shock and horror on the faces of my parents, grandparents and neighbours as the media reported the police findings. To this day, despite numerous searches, one of the bodies has not been found, much to the despair of the family.

Every time I drive on the motorway and come near Saddleworth Moor, I think of those kids whose lives were taken to commit the "perfect crime", as one of the psychopaths proudly confessed when arrested. Thinking of these children for a few seconds is my way of paying tribute to them. I believe that one never forgets such significant events and somehow, I believe that one should not forget.

It is almost with tears in my eyes that I note with relief that I have passed Manchester and the traffic is suddenly more fluid.

Glasgow the beauty of the north! I have only visited Florian a few times, but each time I loved walking around this very attractive city. Glasgow looks out over the Atlantic, it is both bourgeois and working-class. Less wealthy than Edinburgh, it is undeniably much more attractive to my eyes. It is located in the Scottish Lowlands, on the banks of the River Clyde. Of medieval origin, it is the largest city in Scotland, with world-renowned universities. It gave birth to several music groups that have since become internationally famous, such as Simply Minds, Travis and the Knopfler brothers who founded Dire Straits. Glasgow has been designated UNESCO City of Music since 2008.

One cannot talk about Glasgow without mentioning its different architectural styles. My favourite goes to the brilliant designer Charles Rennie Mackintosh who has lined the city with elegant facades.

After seven hours on the road and 400 miles swallowed at rather high speed, I am quite exhausted and so very happy to park my car in front of Florian's restaurant: L'Antre de

Farinet. It has been a long time since I have driven so far. My back hurts, my hip is stiff, my legs are swollen and I am exhausted. I am not used to sitting for so many hours. In the restaurant I am on my feet from morning to night.

Florian and his wife Johana welcome me with open arms. I have known Florian for ages. For his training he spent a few years in London. That is when he met a pretty blonde with beautiful blue eyes, the sparkling Johana. I have often said to myself that Johana must really have fallen in love at first sight, not that Florian is not attractive, on the contrary he is rather handsome, but to leave the South of England and its magnificent beaches, where she comes from, to settle in a big city in Scotland with a rather capricious climate, you really have to be in love. Sometimes Johana needs to get back to her land and go away for a few days. I understand her, the beaches of Cornwall have a unique charm.

"Hi Daniel!".

"Hello, what a pleasure to be back here in Glasgow!".

"I am in a hurry; I have an important banquet to prepare at the restaurant".

Culture obliges, he wears a magnificent kilt. He is deeply attached to his Scottish roots. His guests this evening are representatives of major European travel agencies who organise tours in Scotland.

It will be the beautiful Johana who will take care of me this first evening, which does not displease me. First of all, she is very pleasant to look at, intelligent and easy to converse with, but moreover she knows Marine very well. I will try to get information from her as soon as the opportunity arises.

After showing me the guest room in their large flat above the restaurant, we go down to the bar next to the kitchen. Partaking of a mature whisky, Johana has really good taste, we chat nicely. She tells me about her life in Scotland, the children growing up too fast, Florian's busy job, her own professional involvement in the restaurant, the bookkeeping, the stress.

The restaurant is crowded, we decide to stay at the bar. The food is of course delicious. Unfortunately, the conversation with Johana, which is very interesting by the way, does not give me the opportunity to talk about Marine. It is however a golden opportunity; I will not be alone with her often during my stay. The children are with their grandparents, but they will come back tomorrow. Yet I do not dare interrupt our conversation, which has taken a completely different turn. The moment is so pleasant that I do not want to break the mood. And deep down I know that if Johana tells me what I am afraid of, that Marine is getting married, it will clearly make me miserable. I know myself too well, I will be in a killing mood to hide my pain.

After a few hours, I go to bed without having a single answer to my many questions. Resigned, I believe that sometimes it is better to stay in the dark. Letting the imagination run wild is sometimes preferable to harsh reality.

❋

In the following days Florian leaves his restaurant in the hands of his Head Chef. We spend every afternoon walking in the hills around Glasgow. The scenery is breathtakingly beautiful, the light exceptional. I had almost forgotten the incomparable charm of Scotland.

One morning we take the motorway east to admire the Kelpies, 98 feet high horse-head steel sculptures depicting shape-shifting water spirits, located between Falkirk and Grangemouth. I find these amazing!

We also walk in the city of Glasgow, dine in a different restaurant every day and drink delicious different sorts of whisky. Every night I sleep like a baby.

This stay in the North is very invigorating. I feel good here, the local people are welcoming, the air is pure, although the cold is biting and I am often out of breath.

In the restaurant, Florian shows me his new dishes. In view of our cordial understanding I even dare to ask him the question that haunts my nights and days: "By the way, how do you prepare the Fendant sauce here in Scotland?".

Florian looks at me astonished: "We use the traditional recipe. Why are you asking?".

"Oh, it is because sometimes I have the impression that it is cooked differently depending on the region".

Well, at least I tried. I find it hard to forget that I have not yet found the solution to this enigma and even here, miles away from London, I cannot help but think about it.

We spend the last afternoon of my stay in the kitchen of the restaurant. Florian shows me how to prepare typical Scottish dishes. Of course, the famous haggis, which is the traditional dish of the region, is one of them. It was very popular in the 18th century. Today it usually consists of mutton offal - lungs, liver, heart - onions, oats, kidney fat, spices and salt. Traditionally, this preparation is enclosed in a sheep's belly and cooked for a few hours, making the haggis look like a balloon. Nowadays, it is cooked in a synthetic gut.

So many pleasant moments I will take with me to London, this stay is marvellous! Scotland and my friends give me a taste of life again. I sleep a lot and eat so well that my trousers are a bit tight around the waist. Even my daily headache is gone.

I have not been able to find out about Marine's life. Maybe I am starting to forget her? No, I do not think so. It is impossible.

I even resist the temptation to call Gaston to check what is going on in The Yucca.

It is with bursts of laughter and enjoying an excellent whisky that we end my last evening in Glasgow, then go to bed. Tomorrow the departure will be at dawn.

✳

"Florian, why on earth did Daniel spend a few days in Scotland?".

"My dear and tender wife Johana, it did not escape your attention that he needed a holiday. I just offered him one. I bet he asked you about Marine?".

"I did not give him the opportunity; I did not stop hooking him up with other subjects. It took me years to understand that she is an unhealthy manipulator with perverse tendencies. He does not know that I have been out of touch with her for ages. She has hurt many of my friends, I am still upset about it. I do not know what is going on in her head, but I believe she is a very sick woman. How can anyone be so bad and sadistic? Daniel never suspected the true personality of this horrible Marine".

"No, not for a second. Right, off to bed! Tomorrow, he is leaving, I hope this stay has done him good and that he takes a step back and rests. His life in London is driving him nuts".

After a heartfelt and friendly farewell, I get behind the wheel.

As I arrive at the motorway entrance, I sigh thinking of the many hours of driving ahead of me. I wish I was already home. I wonder how Gaston managed The Yucca while I was away. Selfishly, I hope above all that I will soon discover his recipe for the Fendant sauce.

CHAPTER 28

Two hours after leaving Glasgow the traffic is heavy with trucks blocking the expressway. I am lucky to live and work in London, distances are of little importance. Florian travels by plane when he comes to visit us or when he is on Jake's TV show. He has no problem flying. I am terrified on an aeroplane. If I had been invited to China, I would have had to change my mind, but with a lot of whisky or medicine.

Unpleasant tensions appear in my back, I feel a tingling in my legs and yet I have not covered a third of the route. As I am also starting to get hungry, I decide to take a break. A sign for the next motorway exit appears.

A few minutes later I find myself in the middle of the countryside. After about two miles, I discover a very nice village made up of thatched cottages. So charming! At the end of the main street, I spot a sign indicating a restaurant nearby.

As I enter the building I do not notice much, the interior is rather dark with low beams and small windows. Originally it was probably a barn. An imposing man is standing in front of me. I cannot see his face; my eyes are dazzled by the outside sun and are not yet accustomed to the darkness. According to the clothing of the man it is the chef. I feel relieved, now we are talking!

"Hello, I am the starred Chef Daniel of The Yucca restaurant in London and I would like to eat your best dish".

Not waiting for an answer, I sit down at a table in a corner where I can observe the kitchen, a professional habit. When the door opens, I see microwave ovens. I cannot believe my eyes; I am not going to eat a meal cooked by these! I hate microwave ovens!

A few minutes later, the chef comes back. When he places the dish in front of me, I almost faint. It is simply filthy, shapeless and terribly smelly. I cannot even identify what is on the plate. I raise my head. The chef, immense, with an unappealing look on his face, is standing in front of me. My eyes have grown accustomed to the inside, I can see him clearly now. His cheeks are red, thinning brown hair, his clothes are stained.

He says in a very unsympathetic tone: "So how does the great chef Daniel find my food?".

I am taken aback: "Do we know each other?".

He laughs in a threatening manner, then adds: "Eat every last crumb, I want to see you lick the plate, otherwise my friends at the bar will not let you go".

As I look towards the bar, I see three men nonchalantly sitting on the stools. Otherwise, the restaurant is empty. These three men are as tall, sturdy and strong as the cook and look at me with faces indicating their desire to break my bones. In front of them are big glasses of beer, most of them half-empty, and no doubt not very fresh, neither the beer nor the men.

I feel trapped. Not really understanding what these people want from me, but I guess it is nothing good, I taste the food. It is awful, I cannot help but make a face.

❀

The nightmare lasted three hours. This chef forced me to eat disgusting dishes that he prepared with obvious sadism. At the end of the meal, I am feeling horribly sick.

"So, do you recall now who I am?".

"No, I do not know who you are, I am sorry".

"I am Marcel, the kitchen helper you mistreated and fired many years ago. I had a colleague named Toby. Lucky me! You just happened to stop by my restaurant today and you are paying for all the damage you have done".

I had not recognised him; he has changed a lot. After the not so nice encounter with Toby at the competition in London-Bourg, now my path crosses Marcel. What a pity! I fired them before the end of their contract and if I remember correctly on a not quite honest pretext, but I could not stand this Marcel any more. Not only was he not very good as a chef, but he was also making a big mess, pulling everyone down. Toby was much better at his job, promising, I could have made an effort, but he got carried away by Marcel's nonsense and unfortunately, he was part of the exit package.

During these long and painful hours of real culinary torture I suffered the worst in my life. After swallowing this food, which was not food at all, I was taken out of the restaurant by Marcel's friends without my feet touching the ground and thrown like an old bag on the gravel of the car park. All the content of my stomach was vomited in the dustbin in front of the restaurant.

※

My head is pounding, my stomach, my whole digestive system is on fire. I even have back pains. However, I jump into my car with what little energy I have left to get away from these horrible people.

As I get back on the motorway quite traumatized, I tell myself that I am not safe from running into one of my ex-employees that I mistreated in the past and, like Marcel, he or she may decide to take revenge. I shudder with horror at the idea that it could happen again.

I just understood a crucial lesson. Sooner or later, you pay for your behaviour of the past and it can hurt a lot.

CHAPTER 29

After five hours of driving without stopping, I am worn out. Back in The Yucca with a pounding headache and my stomach still turned over from the stinking food I had to eat, I inspect the place thoroughly. The restaurant was very well kept, clean, impeccable, full of fresh products. Nothing to complain about.

Still in a positive attitude, of wanting to change one's life for the best and loving everybody, Gaston, who was in the courtyard when I arrived, welcomes me with open arms and singing! I look at him twice, not believing my eyes. He is wearing wide clothes, trousers that aren't really trousers, sandals on his feet, all items of a pronounced orange colour, not at all appropriate for a starred restaurant. I open my mouth to complain, but he hugs me tightly. I try as hard as I can to get out of his embrace, but he is taller than me, has more muscles in his arms. He even kisses me again on both cheeks in front of the whole staff, which makes me very uncomfortable! I am afraid that Gaston's new view of professional relations will make me completely lose my authority over my staff.

To escape him, I take refuge in the kitchen corner occupied by Benedict, muttering a remark "about men kissing men and not really being men".

In a split second, everyone freezes, all shocked. I do not understand why my remark makes them so uncomfortable. I am full of flaws but far be it for me to judge anyone on their sexual orientation. Ashamed of my stupid remark, I go home feeling bad and exhausted.

The heavy traffic does not improve my mood, nor my tiredness. I think the whole benefit of my invigorating stay in Scotland has gone up in smoke after my encounter with Marcel.

Finally, after what seemed like an endless journey in London's busy rush hour traffic, I reach the underground carpark of the building where my flat is located. I park my car in my reserved space. I grab my luggage and hear a suspicious cracking sound in my back. The pain is sudden, intense, dazzling, I do not dare to move, my breath is cut off. I let go of my luggage which falls heavily to the ground.

The light goes out after two minutes, it is pitch dark. My back is so painful that I cannot move. Fortunately, I see a neighbour approaching and ask him for help. Unfortunately, this neighbour is one of those who are quite disturbed when I listen to Vivaldi music in the middle of the night. His response is far from diplomatic and polite. He walks away without a glance after a few insults.

After a superhuman effort I manage to move a little. Enduring terrible pain in my back I arrive at my flat. I call the emergency doctor on duty and describe my state. He replies that he will come as soon as possible. Knowing our health care system, it can take hours. My medicine cabinet is desperately empty, no painkillers. I call Gaston and explain the situation. Far from helping me, he advises me to breathe deeply and stay positive. I am furious at his answer, how can you stay positive when the pain is unbearable and you can no longer move! I feel like my back has been cut in half and my lungs compressed. I know already that unless a miracle happens, I will not be able to go to work tomorrow and inform Gaston about it. He tells me not to worry, to listen to my body, and hangs up. I am furious!

After endless minutes, which turned into hours, finally someone rings the doorbell. I open the door in a very bad mood. It is the GP on emergency home calls. I tell him that I do not understand why a personality like me had to wait so long in an extremely painful state. He is a man of about 35 years old, who looks at me with a tired look, large dark circles around his eyes.

After an examination, he informs me that I am probably suffering from lumbago. He gives me an injection and prescribes sessions with an osteopath. Later, when the crisis is over, he adds. The diagnosis will have to be confirmed by further examinations, which I do not intend to carry out. I will be back on my feet in no time.

Moreover, he informs me that it will not be possible to go back to work for a few days. I must remain calm, relax, try to move slowly in my flat, but in no way drive or stand too long on my legs. I am furious at this guy who sees me as a disabled person, is he competent? He prescribes me a long list of medication to fetch from the drugstore, before leaving without saying good-bye. No lost love between us!

How am I going to get the medication if I cannot move? I call the only person who will help me: Lilly.

I dial her mobile number. To my surprise, she answers in an icy tone that she is very busy. I hang up after giving her the order to come as soon as possible. I resent her for taking such a low revenge. All right I ignored her calls when I was in Scotland, but deep down she should be flattered to share the bed with a personality like me, she should have come to my rescue straight away! But no, this ungrateful woman told me she did not have time!

❋

I find myself alone in my flat. I cannot yell at anyone to let off steam. What is more, I fully realise that when the injection no longer takes effect, I am going to suffer martyrdom. An unattractive perspective.

In a sudden vision, it becomes clear to me that my crazy life, my irrational love for my professional activity has made me act relatively often in an uncontrolled way. It is a vicious circle, the more I worked, the more successful I became, but in return the more I became a fool.

Alone in my flat, with my back hurting and unable to move, I experience a great moment of lucidity and solitude.

CHAPTER 30

After an unusual, but much appreciated, twelve hours sleep I wake up feeling better. My back is still sore, but I tell myself that this misadventure is over. Against the orders of the doctor, who was not very competent, I decide to go to work.

As I get dressed, I ignore the increasing pain in my back. I pick up my car keys, in a split second the excruciating pain is back. It is unbearable. Tears come to my eyes. I can barely move my arm, which remains horizontal. I can neither turn to the right nor to the left. It feels like the pain goes all the way down to my toes. Like a robot I try to move around. With great difficulty I reach my mobile phone on the table and call the emergency doctor.

This time the doorbell rings a few minutes later to my great relief. When I open the door, I am taken aback. The man standing in front of me looks very young, like a teenager wearing old jeans and a white tee-shirt, clean shaven but with uncombed hair.

"Where is the doctor who visited me yesterday?".

He answers in a relaxed voice: "Hello, I am Dr Lloyd. My colleague you met yesterday does not want to see you anymore".

I guess my bad mood has made another victim.

I can hardly lie down to be examined by this young man. He is much more talkative than his colleague, asks a lot of questions, some of which I find incongruous, for example if I do any sport. I answer in a voice that reflects my bad mood, that I am running around all day long! He replies that this is not a sport to relax, then asks me if I do any exercise to work my abs; "because the fat on your stomach is not foreign to your back pain", he tells me in a light tone.

I almost choke on the nerve of this young man; I am not fat! To top it all, he ends by asking me if I meditate. Looking at my face, he concludes that I do not and notes it carefully in his notebook.

Unfortunately, the doctor informs me, as I did not follow the wise advice of his colleague, what happened is that my condition has worsened and I am suffering from a compression of the sciatic nerve. Given the new situation it will probably take a week of medication before I can hope to be on my feet again.

"Then an X-ray or maybe a CT scan will be necessary to make a definite diagnosis".

"Who do you think you are? I am very strong and everything will soon be back to normal. I find it hard to understand your pessimism!".

"The visit to the osteopath and the further examinations will have to wait. You cannot move at the moment", he adds.

"THAT I noticed! You are a genius!".

After giving me an injection, he leaves me alone.

As I have nothing left in the pantry, only a lonely old pot of Marmite, I call Gaston to kindly arrange meals to be delivered. I find this phone call difficult, humiliating, in spite of my Head Chef's good mood. I imagine him hanging up the phone and in a thunderous voice throughout the kitchen announcing that I will stay home for a few days, no doubt to the great happiness and relief of the staff.

※

Gaston lets out a long sigh of relief as he rests the handset. Acting constant cheerfulness begins to seriously wear him out!

"So how is he?".

"Benedict, I think what we have feared for a while has just happened. His back is hurting and he can hardly move. He is in a killing mood, which must not help. The emergency doctor has prescribed medication and a week's rest".

"As for whether he will be able to stay home for seven days, I do not believe it for a second!".

"Well, I have to prepare the next part of my plan, because like you I do not think he is going to last a week without showing up. He will have a nasty surprise that will finish him off".

Then Gaston explains his idea to Benedict and Boris. They both listen, eyes and ears wide open.

At the end of Gaston's talk, a silence settles in. Then Benedict says: "You are completely mad!".

"I am going to change the locks of my office door, because this time he is going to blow it up". Boris has just spoken. He has gone all pale.

✳

The kitchen helper who brings my first meal is terrified. He is shaking, almost hooks his foot on the carpet and spills everything. It is true that I have not been kind to him in the past. He must have lost a bet for being designated meal delivery boy to the great monster that I am.

After delivering the meal he could not have got out of my flat any quicker. I do not suffer from the plague by the way!

I gave him my medication prescription. He will get the medicine from the drugstore and will bring it back with the evening meal. At least this is organised! I feel relieved.

✳

In my condition everything is difficult. Forty eight hours since the doctor's visit and I am plying myself with medication, but I do not see much improvement. I even had trouble brushing my teeth this morning, raising my right arm feels like torture. I have to learn how to use my left hand and arm, for a right-handed person this is not easy. I feel diminished, it is humiliating.

An idea crossed my mind this morning when I called Gaston. I asked him to cook my pan-fried foie gras for lunch. It will be accompanied by his famous Fendant sauce. Stuck at home I will have all the time I need to taste it slowly in order to discover the mystery ingredient.

But I am heartbroken when the dish arrives and a new kitchen helper, designated delivery boy for the angry wolf, informs me in a trembling voice that it was not Gaston who cooked the meal, but Robert the recently hired junior chef.

This rascal Gaston must have guessed my intention!

After lunch, there is nothing to do in my flat; nothing to read, no desire for television, no phone calls, deafening silence, and no news of Lilly who is not in her office when I try to reach her. Frankly, she could make an effort, I am not just anyone, I am The Chef Daniel! Few women have the opportunity to be around me. She is so ungrateful!

CHAPTER 31

THREE DAYS, THREE DAYS, that I am confined to my home! I am on the verge of a nervous breakdown. The curtains closed; in the half-light I decide to take a nap curled up on the sofa of the living room. Given the dose of medication I ingested, it is not difficult to fall asleep anywhere and anytime.

Suddenly I am woken up by a strange noise and light invading the room. With a start I open my eyes and see an unknown woman standing in front of me. As surprised as I am, she screams. It is with shame that I notice that I have also screamed out in fear at the sight of her. After an awkward silence during which we stare at each other like two frightened animals, I understand it must be the cleaning lady. I had not recognised her since I had not seen her for a long time and apparently, she did not remember what I looked like either. Clearing my throat, I explain that I am her boss and that I am at home because I am ill. I repeat my sentences several times. Either her language skills are limited or she is too shocked to find me here and cannot concentrate.

Finally, she nods and goes to work without smiling. I am disturbed by this intrusion. She does not seem happy either, but we have to live together for a few hours. With the noise that the cleaning lady makes for once I feel compassion for my neighbours. If the walls are not very soundproof, contrary to what I believed, I do not even dare to imagine what I had put them through in the middle of the night with

Vivaldi music booming when they needed to sleep. The medication gives me a headache, all sounds make it worse. Needless to say, the hubbub of the hoover that my cleaning lady turned on resounds furiously in my skull. I feel unable to move in order not to irritate the migraine a bit more, just turning my head is painful. My back cannot stand any movement, I feel like a stone, heavy and useless.

I resign myself to not moving and stare at the wall in front of me, painfully waiting for the damn hoover to shut up. My morale is starting to play tricks on me. When I look at my flat, I find it dull, ugly, without great quality. A quick glance at my interior gives me the impression that I have no taste, that I have never taken the time to furnish my home in such a way that it feels cosy. Moreover, a new coat of paint on the walls would not be a luxury. Stuck on my sofa, it is as if I am seeing my flat for the first time.

The front door slams, the cleaning lady has left, without saying a word. Did I traumatise her too? Another victim of my bad mood? Probably.

✳

I spend the next few days lying on the sofa, watching uninteresting TV shows. When I come across national and international news I wonder if the world we live in is nothing but violence and nonsense? Then I watch a programme about the horrible story that happened in France, in Paris, and which, too busy with my job, I had not heard about. I must be the only one in all Europe to learn so late about the cartoonists executed in their Paris office by trigger-happy maniacs for unclear ideological reasons. How can a drawing make you lose your life? If I do not like the squeaky humour of Britain's cartoonists, I simply ignore them.

I much prefer to work in the kitchen of my restaurant, even if the atmosphere is sometimes heavy. Ironically, I tell myself that I hope never to take a bullet because I cooked a dish that does not suit one of my guests. Watching the news, I realise that I really have a good life, but that unfortunately we are not immune from the act of a nutcase when we do a public job.

My mood does not get any better when I watch a new cooking show in which Jake is involved. Always smiling, very handsome, Jake prepares his dish with incredible expertise in front of the cameras. It is a great classic of popular British cuisine, fish and chips. But prepared by Jake, it looks like a 3 Michelin star recipe. This show is bound to be another success for my friend, once more, nailed by the pain on my sofa I can see it.

Despite my hard work, I come to the conclusion that my friend is doing much better than I am. Not only am I currently out of action, I have not discovered the mystery of Gaston's Fendant sauce, but also the writing of my book is at a standstill, inspiration is sorely lacking. Not to mention Marine and all the other crap I had to deal with for a while.

I call Jake to congratulate him. He is of course cheerful on the line and asks me how I am. I take a deep breath and tell him all about my misfortune. He replies that once he was unable to work for almost three weeks. I am taken aback; I knew nothing about this. He goes on telling me that he does gymnastics every week and works on his abs to avoid having to endure such a bad experience again. He advises me to do the same.

I listen to him with confusion. I have always assumed that my physical activity at work was enough for my body. And how could I find the time in my overloaded diary to do sport? I never would have thought of Jake doing exercises to relax his body, I thought he hated all sporting activities!

As he rests the handset Jake feels that his cheeks have turned pink and his smile has disappeared. But how could he talk such nonsense to Daniel and without flinching? He hates all forms of sport and has never had a sore back in his life.

Pensive, he looks out the window. It has been years since Daniel changed for the worse. First there was his relationship with that awful Marine who demolished him, then he drowned in work and, to hide his pain, became angry and unbearable. Is he suffering from burnout? If it is the case Jake would not be surprised with the crazy life Daniel has led in recent years.

He misses his friend, the one he knew when they were young. At that time Daniel was a nice guy who had a good sense of humour. Today his anger is constant and he scares the hell out of you, you never know how he will react. A time bomb ready to explode!

Thoughts are racing through Jake's head. Maybe with this current health problem Daniel will ask himself the right questions about the meaning of his life? That would be a good thing.

Jake wonders if he himself is in danger. His life is only a carousel of work, from morning to night he runs in all directions. Has he himself changed for the worse, like Daniel? He prefers not to answer this question.

He suddenly must lean against the wall, he just had a loss of balance, an unpleasant dizziness. It is not the first time. He will have to resign himself to consulting his GP. But when?

With a sigh, he goes back to work.

CHAPTER 32

After 10 days of high doses of medication and complete rest, I begin to notice some improvement. After my bad experience due to my impatience, I follow the doctor's advice and do not move more than necessary.

To my great surprise, the doctor visits me without prior warning. He does not seem afraid of my, shall we say, difficult or strong character, unlike most people. He even manages to joke about it: "You look like an ogre, but I can handle you. I have seen worse!".

Has he really? In a moment of lucidity, I do not dare to imagine what this young man must be going through during his home visits and I almost feel sorry for him.

Fortunately, he finds that my health condition has improved. I might be allowed to return to work in a few days, if I am wise, he adds mischievously.

Then, sitting on the edge of the sofa, he gets into a discussion that I have to put up with, being nailed by my aching back on the same sofa.

"You have to take care of yourself".

"I do. I love my job".

He shakes his head: "You do not understand, your job is not your whole life, it is just a professional activity. You should think about who you really are, what you like to do as a hobby and about your private life".

Then he recommends some exercises to "reduce the fat on my belly" in order to strengthen my abs. These would relieve the pressure on the spine. I feel like wringing his neck. How dare he talk to me again about my so-called fatness?

After a while the doctor leaves. I almost find myself regretting his departure, I note a little bitterly that his visits were the only ones I had apart from the unfortunate terrorised kitchen helpers who deliver the meals and the cleaning lady who screamed in horror to find me home.

※

In the afternoon, I call Gaston to inform him of the good news that I will soon be back at work. I am told that he is not at the restaurant. I am annoyed and look at my watch, he should be in at this time, but where can he be? Benedict is hastily put on the phone. He is as usual in an imperturbable mood and informs me that Gaston is at his yoga class.

I am shocked. "WHAT? Is Gaston allowing himself to go to a yoga class during working hours?". I bark into the receiver.

"Yes, and it is not the first time, in fact he goes three times a week". Benedict hangs up with a sigh.

Gaston's crisis after having made me smile a little at first has become a serious problem for the smooth running of the establishment. Yoga classes during working hours! I rant, I cannot stand this! Against the doctor's advice, with difficulty, I get dressed, determined to go to The Yucca to put things in order. Deep down inside I know I am making a huge mistake, but I cannot contain my fury.

※

Hiding in Boris' office, Benedict looks at his friend.

"Gaston, I bet he will be here in a few minutes. In my opinion you have gone too far. I think this time he is going to blow a fuse and I doubt he will like the new decorations".

"Do not worry Benedict, I know exactly what I am doing. Trust me, for the moment my plan is working perfectly".

※

Drugged and a bit wobbly, walking slowly with one hand on my hip, I enter the restaurant. The pain is agonising, I am clenching my teeth.

If I had managed to stay more or less calm until then, the bomb explodes when I enter the main dining room. I discover, with horror and amazement, Buddha statues instead of my beautiful and precious Yucca trees!! A crime of lèse-majesté. This time I am going to kill Gaston. This crazy situation has gone on long enough. No one touches my precious plants. I YELL to put my Yucca trees back in their special places. My employees are running around in terror.

In a killer's mood, blinded by rage, I look for the culprit. I find him in the kitchen, which quickly empties itself of its occupants. The two of us remain alone face to face, like gladiators in the lions' den. A merciless fight is brewing. My opponent, all dressed in orange clothes, stares at me not at all frightened.

My hand on my back I am trying to calm the stabbing pain that almost takes my breath away. The tension is so palpable in the room that the air has become unbreathable. And I EXPLODE.

I YELL at him. The frustration of my immobility of the last few days explodes in broad daylight. I yell at him at the top of my voice. One probably hears me all the way to Brixton Tube Station.

The vocal orgy lasts for long minutes. Gaston faces me without moving.

At the end of my indecent outburst, he stares at me and then without uttering a word leaves the room.

The pain in my back is unbearable, I bend forward. I cannot stand up straight anymore, tears come to my eyes. The Fendant sauce is on a plate where Gaston was only a few minutes ago. I taste it and once again it is exceptional.

I go home dragging my leg. In my car, driving has become difficult, my back is screaming in pain, tears are running down my cheeks. Never in my life have I suffered so much physical pain! It is like having my body pierced with scissors.

Back in my apartment I call the medical emergency service. A few moments later the practitioner who had already taken care of me in the morning shows up. He is cheerful and shows signs of sympathy towards me. It is incomprehensible that this guy manages to put up with me with a smile when I am so irritable with others. And I am no better with him, I am almost insulting him, my nerves are getting the better of me. But he examines me pretending not to notice my slaughtering mood.

He gives me an injection which, although painful, quickly relieves my pain. My bad mood suddenly goes away. And as if he was used to it, this young doctor sits down on the edge of the sofa and asks me in a soft voice: "What happened to put you in such a state?".

This skinny, teenager looking guy, thinks he is my shrink! It annoys me tremendously and I want to wring his neck, but a quick calculation makes me realise that my arms would not reach him. He sits cautiously at the other end of the sofa.

I am not going to get rid of him with small talk and as I have found that my wrath has no impact on him, I let go. As the pain eases, I find myself telling him what happened, a story a little embellished for my benefit, but all is said without forgetting the fact that I treated my faithful Gaston like an idiot.

He listens to me attentively, then he says: "I am appalled, you are really an unbearable ogre and an enigma to me! You are doing the job you have always dreamed of, you have reached the highest level, you are surrounded by a competent team, but you are ruining it all! Go on, tell me everything!".

I am old enough to be his father, but without much effort he manages to make me confess all my faults, even the least glorious ones. But it must be said that he has a formidable weapon. His shot of medication quickly did its job and just with the pain gone, my gratitude is such that I obey and here I am telling him about my life!

Of course, at the end of the story of the disaster of the last few weeks I do not escape his advice. With the voice of a university professor scolding a student, he recommends that I apologise to Gaston, open up to him and listen to what he has to say.

Then he leaves adding that we will probably see each other again soon, because he does not believe I am yet ready to make any significant changes in my life, that I still have not understood anything and that I will soon need a new injection.

He annoys me. But somehow, I feel he is right, despite my reluctance. Although I think about it for a few moments, I still do not get what he means by what I "need to understand to make the necessary changes in my life to stop this back pain". What does he want me to change in my life? It is perfect! In a sigh I stop thinking about it. Probably this is a youthful whim on the part of this doctor, a trendy new trick. Anyway, I am the great starred Chef Daniel and no one can take that away from me. I am not going to change; I am the way I am and I am going to stay that way!

Moralising speeches never suited me, whether they came from my parents or the teachers. Only my grandmother could make herself heard. With a twinge in my heart, I wonder what she would say about my situation. This thought makes me very uncomfortable; I feel tears coming to my eyes. I cruelly miss my dear granny, her passing away has left an emptiness that has never been filled. She was my mentor, a beacon in this ocean of life. But the lighthouse went out leaving me all alone. I am drowning.

CHAPTER 33

The next morning, sprawled out on the living room sofa and already bored to death, the ringing of the phone comes as a surprise and a pleasant distraction.

It is Michael. He hardly greets me, goes straight to the point. Following his experience at the Shanghai Meridien, he is organising a special evening at the Saillon Manoir. He will cook Chinese dishes for his close friends, VIPs and of course some of the journalists of the written press, including the well-known Jules. "I am counting on your presence", he adds.

Before I can open my mouth to inform him about the pitiful state, I am in, he enthusiastically talks about the dishes he is working on and, he is certain, will be a success during the evening and later on will further enhance the restaurant's fame. Michael does not lack self-confidence, after only a few days in Shanghai, here he is proclaiming himself a great chef of Chinese cuisine! My legendary jealousy is back in a split second.

He goes on by pointing out that the dishes in question are traditionally presented during the Chinese New Year. As this meal is considered the most important of the year, great rigour is required in its preparation.

He explains, like the connoisseur he has suddenly become, that it is extremely difficult to choose dishes because the variety is so vast. However, he adds almost modestly, he will cook the following recipes; for the traditional *Nianyefan* meal, meaning the "cold" dishes typical of Shanghai: *sixikaofu*, then *maodou* and *jiangya*. The main course will be a *yanduxian* with *babaofan*, as well as *ganlancai* and *bingtangyangrou*.

I am on the verge of freaking out. He does not even bother to describe the composition of these supposedly great dishes. And by the way I do not understand a word of Chinese!

I am beginning to feel very irritated. Immediately the back pain intensifies. I make a superhuman effort to calm down, realising that if I get angry the pain will not spare me, on the contrary.

When I finally get the opportunity to stop Michael's speech, I tell him about my misadventure. In a calm voice I explain that I have been bed-ridden for a few days and in great pain. It is unthinkable that I will be on my feet for his party which will take place in forty eight hours. I make it clear how much I would prefer to be part of it. I apologise, even though I am the one to suffer from this situation.

This cuts off Michael's stream of words and a heavy silence sets in. For a few seconds I wonder if he is still on the line. Then in a cold voice he asks me to repeat the fact that I will not be able to make it to his special invitation. He specifies, now a little hostile, that he really counts on my presence and says he is extremely disappointed.

I repeat again that I am very sick and that in normal circumstances I would not have missed his invitation, but that the situation really does not depend on me. Although I am very touched by his phone call and am infinitely grateful to him, I am simply too ill.

Michael hangs up. He has not even asked me what happened.

I am stunned. I look at the phone as it beeps indicating that the conversation is over. Michael's tone became cold as soon as I told him I had to decline his invitation. Normally, I would not think any further and would quickly go back to work, but as I am stuck at home and cannot move, I start to think about my friendship with Michael.

I admire him, maybe too much. It suddenly jumps out at me that I have always done what he wants and it is with some uneasiness that I realise that I "obey" Michael. I always put his wishes before mine.

Painfully, as I delve into my memory, I recall episodes that make me uncomfortable. Michael had not managed to make it to the inauguration of The Yucca when I was counting on his presence. He is always interested in my recipes, without revealing his. My friendship with Michael goes back a long way, to when we were young kitchen helpers. On many occasions I helped Michael without him returning the favour. Why have I acted this way? The answer is quite obvious, he has power and influence. I unconsciously fear him a little. When he lost Le Coralie, his first restaurant, he became so angry that he scared the hell out of all of his friends. Still does to this day.

Michael's reaction was icy and not very empathetic as soon as I "disobeyed" him, even though it is by no means my fault if I am too ill to go to his party. I cannot help but compare what just happened with the phone call I made to Jake, who was concerned about my condition and listened to me.

＊

An uneasiness has invaded Michael. He spoke to his friend a few hours ago and cannot forget that conversation. Is Daniel really sick? Michael does not believe it for a second. Why did he refuse his invitation? He knows full well that Daniel is jealous of him and would have loved to have been invited to China instead of him. Maybe he has not digested it?

Is his friend flouting their friendship? Michael feels his heart squeeze. He knows about betrayal. Since he lost Le Coralie, he finds it hard to trust anybody even his long-time friends.

＊

I do not know if it is the medication, or my immobility, but despite my best efforts, I cannot get my discussion with Michael out of my head. Even though I try, nothing helps, I cannot concentrate on anything else.

This discussion with Michael made me realise that my friends may not really be my friends. Are they loyal? Doubts overwhelm me. Would they help me if I was in trouble? Would they support me if I had problems at the restaurant? What if I lose a star? A perspective that gives me shivers of horror.

Gaston refuses to talk to me on the phone. I cannot believe it! He holds quite a grudge. It is Benedict who, in a voice as placid and calm as ever, gives me news. When I ask if the customers are worried about my absence, Benedict tells me that they are not, even though they are informed that I am bedridden.

I bitterly regret, and let it be known harshly, that information about my health is leaked out to customers, it cannot be good for my reputation. What if the famous Mr Tornado shows up and learns that I am unwell? That could be a disaster. Being in good health is paramount in my business. At the end of our conversation, I dare to ask him if Gaston is mad at me, he sighs and replies before hanging up: "More than ever".

"You know you are putting me in a difficult situation, you and your crazy ideas! You heard me lying to the boss! The customers were worried about his absence and of course we did not say a word about his state of health".

"Do not worry, I know what I am doing".

Despite his reassuring words, Gaston is not so sure. He hopes that everything will work out as planned. In any case, he no longer has a choice. Considering the state in which Daniel presented himself in The Yucca and the horrible, hurtful, words, it is a situation of no return.

CHAPTER 34

It is the understatement of the year to say that I did not sleep well. I was constantly woken up by nightmares. I kept turning over in my bed, which caused me searing pains.

This morning looking at the mirror I see a poor image of myself, dark circles around my eyes, greasy hair and a pale complexion. I do not think I have ever looked so ugly.

During the night my thoughts flared up, my boiling brain gave me no respite. I thought over and over about Michael's phone call, the preparation of the Fendant sauce, the snow that disrupted the running of the restaurant, the incident with The Beauties, Lilly, Marine, the countess, Gaston who refuses to talk to me, the customers who do not seem to notice my absence and the misadventure with Marcel who made me eat filthy dishes. Even the memory of the competition and the attitude of the half-Swiss chef Toby came back to my mind without mentioning Mr Tornado.

Stuck at home and alone, I have no choice but to think, to cogitate. My back pain has become the boss, I must resign myself to obey it. The slightest annoyance worsens my condition. My usual weapon: anger, has become my worst enemy. Over the years my body has wisely obeyed me. Not anymore. Now it wickedly rebels.

Twenty four hours after Michael's phone call, no matter how hard I try, I cannot forget what happened. To say the least I am disappointed at his reaction. As I have got nothing else to do, I am intrigued to know what my friends really think of me. Putting my pride aside, I decide to call them, just to see their reaction when I tell them about my misadventure. As I pick up the phone, I wonder why it is so important to me all of a sudden to know if I am appreciated. Do I need affection, love, in these moments of loneliness?

Rick answers the phone in a hurry. I tell him about my condition. His reaction pleases me, he bombards me with questions, he seems really concerned. I apologise for disturbing him as he seems really busy. But Rick replies that the potatoes and celery can wait. He then explains that his brother Damian is a physiotherapist in Dorset County where he runs a health centre. He offers to ask him for advice.

I hang up the phone a few minutes later. I did not expect such a reaction from Rick. Of course, we have known each other for years, but I feel uncomfortable. I could have helped Rick on many occasions, but it did not even occur to me. Yet he has taken the time, no doubt precious, to talk to me, listen to me and even proposed his brother's help. I acted with Rick exactly the same way Michael acted with me. I am not proud of it, now I know how much it can hurt to feel used.

Feeling ill at ease I dial Florian's number, because I am very determined to continue what I now call my investigation. The beautiful Johana picks up the phone. She is laughing, in a very good mood. When I explain my condition, her voice becomes very concerned, she shows great humanity, which touches me. She seems seriously worried and concerned about my health. Florian being in town, I cannot talk to him. Johana promises me that she will pass on the message upon his return. After the customary pleasantries and her good wishes for recovery, we say goodbye.

I am a little shaken by Johana's kindness and empathy, which I know to be sincere. I wonder if Florian will call me back or if he will be satisfied with the fact that I have spoken to his wife.

The phone rings, it is Jake. I can hardly believe my ears when I hear his voice. With his busy schedule he is not often free for private calls. As he is the closest of my friends, I tell him openly about the incident at the restaurant and how I treated Gaston. Jake is a bit harsh on the issue and tells me that I must make amends. Gaston is a great chef. He reminds me that I could always count on my Head Chef and that I must speak to him quickly to avoid not only him finding work elsewhere, which would be easy enough for him, but also for the smooth running of the business.

Directly after Jake's call, Florian is on the phone. His swift reaction surprises me. He is very attentive and really concerned about my health.

When I hang up the phone after these various conversations, I am disconcerted. I have got the answer to my questions. But I am not sure I am happy with what I have found out. I feel lousy about my past attitude towards Rick and Florian. Let's be honest, I have always appreciated them, but I also considered them as second-class chefs, who were nice to have as friends, but not very important in my career. It is different with Michael and Jake; I have always put them first on my list. As for Jake, I am not disappointed, although he lectured me about my way of treating Gaston. It is a very different feeling when I think of Michael who clearly showed how little I meant to him. Business and only business. Have I wasted my time with him?

"Florian, I am really worried, look at Daniel's misadventure, he does not seem to realise it, but he has fallen to the bottom of the abyss. You guys really lead a crazy life! Honestly my dear husband, we have to talk about the future, we have to think about our children, I do not want you to become a wreck like Daniel!".

"Do not worry my beautiful wife, when I saw the state he was in when he arrived in Glasgow, I had a shiver of horror. What is happening to him is basically not so bad. He has to rest and I am not fooled that his phone call today is only the beginning. I just hope that one day he will become again the good guy he was before all this madness with the Michelin stars happened and, above all, before he met Marine!".

"Damian, Daniel is bedridden! He is suffering from terrible back pain. I think he has not yet fully understood the state he is in. He just called me and beat around the bush, but I think he wanted to know if our friendship was real! Can you imagine that!".

"Ok, it was to be expected that his health would quickly deteriorate. Now he has to take care of himself and turn his life around. At the moment I bet he is in denial".

"I sincerely hope that he will recover. I told him about your health centre, he said he is interested to learn more about your activities. I will give you his email address, send him a message. You know, I feel guilty because I did not tell him about Marine's character. She regularly cheated on him when they were together. She must not learn that he is sick, she is capable of visiting him to make his life a little more miserable. My friend Hugh had an affair with her and he had a horrible time! What he told me gave me the creeps".

I call back The Yucca and once again Gaston refuses to speak to me. Benedict takes the call. Imperturbable, he gives me news about the restaurant in a linear tone, while adding with disconcerting frankness: "Gaston hates you".

I do not know how to handle this situation and tell Benedict that I apologise to Gaston.

He replies: "I do not want to get involved and if you want to apologise, do it directly with the person concerned".

How can I apologise to someone who refuses to talk to me?

I hang up, very upset.

CHAPTER 35

There is not much to do alone at home. I am bored. At the slightest annoyance or even if I walk a bit fast the back pain becomes unbearable. I move very slowly, much too slowly for me who did not know the word patience before. Such mundane movements as brushing my teeth, taking a shower or getting dressed take time and a pain management strategy. I have become a robot. Pathetic.

I try to distract myself by switching on the television, but after three times zapping all the channels and finding that there is not even a snooker broadcast on the sports channels, I violently throw the remote control against the wall. This angry gesture is enough to wake up the monster in my back, I scream in pain. Tears come to my eyes.

And on top of that the remote control is destroyed, bravo!

I inevitably again start thinking about the events of the last few weeks, even years. It is as if my brain cannot stop turning and turning over what has happened in my life in terms of negative events, what has gnawed at me internally, what I have hidden out of weakness so as not to have to face it, my failures, my humiliating moments. These thoughts drive me nuts. It is like my whole life flashes before my eyes, from my childhood in the countryside to today, that all my memories, the bad ones, the less glorious ones, the humiliations, resurface. I cannot take any more of this brain that cannot shut up. No matter how hard I try to concentrate on my successes, to connect my brain to the moments of glory, to remember the newspaper articles in my favour, nothing helps.

After going around the living room three times, very slowly and with difficulty, I turn on my computer, just to take my mind off my thoughts and get back to writing my cookery book. In front of my manuscript and after some useless and counter-productive prevarications, I realise that inspiration is not there and decide to check my emails. And there is a surprise!

First there is a message from Lilly. In cold terms she ends our relationship. I am surprised to notice a pinch in my heart, did I get a little fond of her?

Then there is an email from Rick's brother, Damian, describing some physical exercises to do regularly. Unbelievable, I can really count on Rick to help me! Once again, I feel terrible about my way of behaving with Rick. Michael's phone call and his cold attitude plunged me into questioning, but the answers to these questions now plunge me into clinical depression.

These new thoughts of an existential nature are starting to seriously mess up my life. Why does all this guilt overwhelm me?

And this back pain that never ends, no improvement, on the contrary I am under the impression it is getting worse.

I go to bed in the early evening, after a horrible day spent thinking about my life which seems to be more a disaster than a success. I feel like I have fallen pretty low. I feel useless and I am frightened.

CHAPTER 36

I wake up suffering from a headache and feeling terribly tired. Again, I had nightmares all night long.

Around 10.00 a.m. I call The Yucca to speak to Gaston, but once again he refuses to talk to me. Benedict sighs helplessly on the other end of the phone. Somewhere deep down inside I understand that Gaston is terribly upset, but the entrepreneur in me is bubbling up to fix this problem and move on. I order my meal, which will be brought by a kitchen helper around 11.30 a.m.

So, I am told.

※

To my great surprise it is not a kitchen helper who brings the meal, but Gaston. When he enters the living room the air becomes unbreathable and heavy. An awkward silence settles in when he puts the tray down on the table.

I sit on the couch. My back hurts so much that I feel like I am being squeezed in a vice.

Then he looks straight at me and says: "You wanted to talk to me?".

Definitely not very friendly, my Head Chef. I get horribly nervous. I sweat and swallow noisily, which makes my discomfort even worse. Gaston is no longer in a Zen attitude. In fact, today, and for the first time in weeks, he is not wearing orange clothes. He is dressed in dark jeans and a white shirt.

I signal him to sit down, but he ignores my gesture. Standing in front of me, Gaston, seen from the far end of my sofa, looks huge. I feel as impressive as a small shrimp. To add to my discomfort, as if that were possible, I realise with horror that this morning I ran out of clean clothes and had to put on an old pair of pink indoor trousers. I do not even know how I can own such an awful piece of clothing!

The physical and mental suffering have taken away my self-confidence. My strength has failed me, my iron will has deserted me. In a few days life has taught me a very harsh lesson.

It does not take a genius to understand why he is here. I start by asking Gaston for forgiveness. I continue by saying that I recognise his immense qualities and his impeccable work, which has always impressed me. I cannot look at him and stare at the floor. I am so ashamed!

He remains silent. Perhaps encouraged by his attitude, I go on talking. Words come out of my mouth without violence, but with frenzy, like a dam that finally breaks under the weight of the water now pouring into the valley. This water, this stream of words, is all I have thought of Gaston over the years of collaboration, thoughts that at this moment are transformed into words. I express everything he represents to me. I relate the times he impressed me, the times I could count on him. The deepest part of myself expresses itself, I do not know why, but as the words come out of my mouth, I feel liberated.

And I also feel pathetic. As I listen to myself, I realise how unfair I have been to my faithful and very precious Head Chef. In recounting the scenes during our life in the kitchen, I do not come out of it grown up, nor human, but a kind of two-headed monster.

At the end of my speech, a heavy silence settles in. I finally dare to raise my head.

Gaston looks at me calmly and then says: "It is a start".

I am taken aback. I did not expect this lack of reaction. I feel a little anger rising inside me.

After suggesting that I eat before the food gets cold, Gaston turns around and leaves my flat.

The meal is obviously cold, but I am starving and eat it fast.

Gaston did not have the expected reaction after my speech, but I feel lighter, I feel like I have lost a few stones. After the tensions, the refusals to talk to me, he came to see me. I feel like a kid who has just received a gift. That fills me with happiness. On reflection, I tell myself that he left my flat less angry than when he arrived. This relieves me, the situation between us weighed on me. Part of me is broken, collapsed. I feel better now. Even my back pain seems to be alleviated.

Gaston is sitting in his car. He does not know how he could listen to his boss's confession while remaining cold and distant. He did not expect such a flood of words.

Unbelievable that Daniel managed to talk so much and so sincerely! Gaston was completely taken aback, not knowing how to react, he did not utter a word.

He now has to move on to the next stage of the plan and with what he has in mind, it could really turn sour, until now it was a piece of cake.

In a moment of weakness, he considers stopping the plan, giving up, but a little voice in the back of his mind advises him to go on, that Daniel has not really understood yet that he has to change, for the good of everybody, of himself, and especially of The Yucca.

He knows that he has the support of Rick, Benedict and Boris, but has not revealed the remaining part of his plan to them, he has not dared. They would take him for a fool, once again.

He also needs to tell Daniel that the situation at The Yucca is very serious, indeed catastrophic, but he does not have the courage to tell him that, not yet.

One detail that Rick mentioned a while ago comes up again and again in his mind. Apparently, Daniel had a great sense of humour before he crossed paths with Marine. What if he manages to awaken this sense of humour that must still be there somewhere? The remaining part of his plan will tell him that.

I am so disturbed by my confession that I do not dare to call the restaurant later on. Doubts invade me again. Why did I talk so much, so openly?

As I do not want my brain to continue to torment me after Gaston's visit, I swallow more medication than necessary before going to bed. I have only one desire, to knock myself out.

When I feel that sleep is winning me over, a horrible thought crosses my mind. At this moment Gaston could be making fun of me, make all the employees laugh by mimicking me in the kitchen of The Yucca.

You never know what can happen with subordinates.

CHAPTER 37

For once, I slept very well, but I woke up feeling awful. I should not have swallowed so many painkillers. I consciously wanted to silence not only my physical pain, but also my mental one.

After a shower, I feel a little better physically, but just as miserable mentally. Sighing, I put the kettle on to make some tea.

Around noon the doorbell rings. It is a kitchen helper bringing my lunch. I am a bit disappointed; I was hoping that Gaston would come and visit me again.

No Fendant sauce on the menu. Pity!

While I observe the employee's attitude with a sharp eye, I feel reassured, no change, still as terrified. Therefore, it is highly probable that my imagination went wild the day before and that Gaston did not report our discussion in unflattering terms, as I had imagined, or rather feared.

The kitchen helper no doubt felt very uncomfortable with my insistence on talking to him and observing him. He ran away.

I feel very lonely. All my friends and acquaintances are at work and I am stuck between my four walls doing nothing. Useless and futile time with no purpose! How fed up I am! How I wish my life could get back to normal! Please whoever is up there in heaven, the joke has gone on long enough, make it stop. The lesson is learned!

✳

I am sprawled on the couch wearing an old jumper that does not suit me at all, it is far too short. After these hours of inactivity, I am on the verge of a nervous breakdown, which has brought back pain in my spine.

Around 5.00 p.m. the doorbell rings.

Gaston is standing in front of me.

I am so happy to see him, that emotion overwhelms me. If I could, I would jump for joy on my two legs and hang myself from his neck. Of course, I do not do that. I no longer understand my reactions and my overflowing emotions. What is happening to me? My thoughts embarrass me.

Unlike the day before, Gaston starts to talk. I hang on his every word, eager to hear what he has to say. But suddenly the doorbell rings. Who is this harmful intruder? I am too eager to hear what my Head Chef wants to tell me.

Gaston opens the door. I recognise the voice of Dr Lloyd: "I am here to see the big bad wolf". Gaston smiles, a surprised look on his face.

After these long days of loneliness, having two visitors in my living room is almost like having a party! Long gone are the social evenings where I snubbed the people who could not bring me anything in terms of business, long gone are the invitations thrown carelessly in the bin because there were too many. I pray today to be on my feet and be able to get out of this flat which has become a prison.

Dr Lloyd is cheerful and joking: "You are an ogre who eats the GP", winking at Gaston.

"Yes, and I love it, I eat a GP every morning for breakfast!".

I am so happy about these visits breaking my solitude that I smile, in a new mood that could not be more sincere. I already feel that I am going to miss those two after they leave and I want to hold them back. I am more and more afraid of being face to face with my thoughts.

After examination and renewing my prescription, Dr Lloyd leaves, not without promising to come back to see me soon with a look that says a lot about the fact that he thinks I am not going to follow his advice.

Gaston seems taken aback by the way I behaved with Dr Lloyd. He observed us with questioning eyes and had difficulty hiding his surprise.

When we are alone again, he begins to speak in a serious voice, his forehead wrinkled, while still standing. He tells me he appreciates what I said yesterday, understands that my speech was sincere and that it was not easy to speak so frankly and so intimately.

This is a diplomatic way of describing my confession.

To my great surprise he adds, in a calm voice, after beautiful sentences that let me glimpse the rainbow of happiness of our rebirth of good relations, that this is not enough. "I want more from you, I want concrete actions, I want you to listen to me, I want you to change your attitude, because I am afraid that once you're back on your feet you'll become the filthy character I know so well".

Gaston barely refrains from adding: I want you to go back to being the person you were before you crossed paths with that awful Marine who hurt you so badly.

I am amazed. Gaston never speaks to me like that. I am mistaken and propose to increase his salary. He shakes his head and refutes that it is not at all what he wants.

Then he tells me his plan.

As I listen, I feel my jaw dropping. I cannot believe my ears!

CHAPTER 38

Back in The Yucca, Gaston has difficulty concentrating on his tasks. Since he left Daniel's flat, he feels sick, nauseous. He explained his plan to his boss. While talking he knew full well that Daniel was never going to accept what he requires. He wanted to push him around, make him think. He hoped that Daniel would burst out laughing, joking, or at worst shouting as he usually does, and that a sincere discussion would follow. But no, against all odds Daniel listened to him without uttering a word. His reaction destabilised Gaston who now feels completely lost.

He wanted Daniel to take his famous plan lightly, not seriously!

He looks around the kitchen and his heart sinks. He loves The Yucca; he really loves working here. Tears come to his eyes. Suddenly he is overcome with doubts and curses himself. He has no desire to go to work elsewhere and has not received a tempting offer from another establishment, contrary to what he told Daniel. He feels bad for all the lies he told in the past few weeks. But did he have a choice? He has been aware for months that his boss is going straight to hit the wall, could he let this happen without reacting?

Far from reassuring him, Benedict and Boris again called him a raving lunatic when he explained what he had proposed to Daniel.

Rick was not any softer on the phone: "You are in BIG trouble, man!".

✻

Gaston left a few hours ago. The plate of supper remained on the table. I am stunned by what he demanded. How did he dare? I am going to be the laughing stock of all London. I cannot bring myself to agree to his damn plan, but Gaston has left me no choice. It is whether I comply, or he resigns. He did not hide the fact that he had received a very attractive proposal to work in a three star restaurant.

I know that everything he told me makes sense to him. But as far as I am concerned, it is unthinkable! How dare he impose such blackmail on me The Great Chef Daniel? Gaston was very clear. I must accept his plan or he quits, resulting in the programmed end of The Yucca. The Yucca without Gaston will not work. Nobody can replace a Head Chef like him.

Benedict is an amazing chef and the staff are excellent, even if I have never told them, I have always thought so. The restaurant could run, but not at its highest level, as it runs today, and I want to keep my two Michelin stars. Without Gaston bye bye the two stars and it is obvious I will never get the third one. The shame, the downfall!

If Gaston leaves, I would have to quickly recruit, train, lose time in short, before returning to the current level of The Yucca. And it is unthinkable that in my state, and even once I am back on my feet, which is not on the agenda given my health condition, I could do without my precious Head

Chef. I simply cannot afford, for the smooth running of The Yucca, for what I have taken so many years to build, for all the money I have invested, to let Gaston go.

✳

Night has fallen, it is midnight. I am still nailed to my sofa in the dark, I did not even think to turn on the light. My thoughts are on what Gaston told me. His words still resonate unpleasantly in my ears. I listened to what he demanded, eyes wide open, without flinching, without daring to interrupt him. No sound could come out of my mouth, no sensible thought could materialise. I did not even protest, too shocked by what I was hearing.

Gaston's proposal is basically simple. Either I obey his instructions to the letter, or he leaves The Yucca.

His demand is nothing more and nothing less than to accompany him to his meditation sessions and yoga classes, and not just once!!! It is unimaginable that The Great Chef Daniel finds himself wearing tights in a room full of lunatics, sitting on the floor and saying Oouuuuummmmmmmm Moooaaahhh with a round mouth and closed eyes!

Just at the thought of it, I feel nauseous. My hands tremble and I blush with horror and shame. I feel like drinking a whole bottle of Cornalin. But I cannot have it, not even a drop of this delicious wine, my body being full of medication, all alcohol is strictly forbidden. I can only think about the situation soberly and face it with increasing anxiety.

※

I spend half the night thinking and developing strategies to get out of this situation. I must at all costs find a way to make Gaston change his mind, it is a matter of survival for my restaurant, keep Gaston, without losing my dignity, without giving in to his odious blackmail. I will not tell my friends what is happening to me. Unthinkable that I would go to these marijuana classes! Maybe I will find a way to blackmail Gaston, he who thinks he is the cleverest of us both? To turn the blackmail against the blackmailer? The idea is not unpleasant.

At dawn, I wake up with a start on the sofa, covered in sweat. I had a nightmare, a horrible one. Dressed in candy-pink outfits, tights that did not hide much, neither my potbelly nor my intimate anatomy, I was in a large room surrounded by women who looked strangely like Lilly and some of my former conquests that I had mistreated. These women laughed at me because I could not put one leg behind my neck. They laughed heartily, then they came menacingly towards me, then attacked me, their hands with long, colourful, sharp nails lacerating my face. Horrible, horrible nightmare! Gaston and his stupid idea ruined a precious night's sleep. As I turned and turned nervously on the sofa in the living room, not at all made to sleep on, my back pain is excruciating.

The pack of medication comes to my rescue. I greedily swallow a few pills. If I listened to myself, I would swallow the contents of the whole pack.

Painstakingly, I move toward the bedroom. Once in bed and before closing my eyes I recall that during the last few hours I had some interesting ideas on how to get out of this blackmail.

Strategy Nr 1: I ask, no I demand, from Gaston that he reveals his recipe of the Fendant sauce while promising to accompany him to one of these classes, then I find good excuses not to go.

Strategy Nr 2: call the doctor, explain the situation and convince him to tell Gaston that yoga and meditation are totally contraindicated in my case.

Strategy Nr 3: find a way to blackmail Gaston, delve into his personal history, his past, something odious that he does not want people to find out about, and then I threaten to reveal it in public. For this I will have to question my friend Rick. But just the idea of involving Rick makes me feel terribly uncomfortable. I have not forgotten his kindness. Have I fallen so low? That would be stabbing Rick in the back and given the recent events I do not feel capable of it, despite all the bad faith that usually characterizes me. I am abandoning strategy Nr 3, just thinking that it crossed my mind makes me feel like a loser. I am ashamed of myself.

Strategy Nr 4: ...... not yet found. But I will be working on it.

✹

I fast fall asleep and only wake up when the doorbell rings at around 11.30 a.m.

It is a kitchen helper, terrified as usual, who brings my lunch, carrying the tray with trembling hands and wobbling every step.

I am drugged by the dose of medication I swallowed and suffer from a horrible headache. But I am hungry. I eat the meal in no time. It is delicious by the way. There are advantages to being fed by chefs working in a starred restaurant. Having come to my senses, and having identified a few strategies to get out of the situation imposed upon me by Gaston, I feel better.

After a cold shower, I get dressed. As I have no desire to spend another unproductive afternoon sprawled out on the sofa watching TV, I start thinking about what I can do that does not make my inner enemy angry again. Carefully moving, I notice that my back "holds". I walk very slowly. However, something is happening, I feel alive again, I feel like I am slowly starting to get better.

With this observation in mind, I turn on my computer and read Damian's email again. It is with this new positive attitude that the time has come to do the exercises mentioned. Little by little, more to keep myself busy, I start to follow the instructions. I am taking my time because I do not want to upset my back.

No wonder Damian gives good advice, he is the director of a well-known health centre in Stourpaine, north Dorset.

While feeling sorry for myself, it did not even cross my mind to thank him for his message. I take a break to communicate my gratitude for his precious advice by informing him that I intend to practice his exercises every day, because I want to be on my feet as soon as possible.

The war against this back pain has started. I spend the next two hours doing the exercises and contrary to what I had imagined, I am having a lot of fun. The inactivity was slowly killing me. Even though my movements are very slow and I walk like a rusty robot, at least I feel like I am doing something for myself, at least I feel like my body is starting to obey me again.

All boosted by these exercises, I feel revived. After feeling that I have done enough, I slowly make my way to the kitchen for a well-deserved refreshing drink before taking a nap.

My spirits are high.

But it does not last.

Suddenly a thought crosses my mind. It falls on me like a ton of bricks and my spirits fall vertiginously into the abyss of clinical depression.

To do some exercises, basically quite simple, I needed two hours and now I feel like someone who has just run a marathon. How can I, in my condition, envisage returning to a normal life and the long hours of stress at work in the near future? In a few weeks my health has deteriorated so much that I cannot even stand on my legs for two hours. The doctor had suggested that I use a walking cane, I wanted to squeeze his throat to even suggest it, but now I believe I will need one.

It will probably take a long time before I can move normally and stand on my legs for hours. Will I ever go back to the way I was before?

I am beginning to understand that the doctor was not joking when he talked about further tests, x-rays and maybe even a CT scan. Something is seriously wrong with my health. It is not normal that there is so little improvement; on the contrary the slightest annoyance only makes my condition worse.

It is suddenly obvious that I am going to be on sick leave for weeks or even months. What seemed unthinkable just slapped me in the face. I no longer have a choice; the illness has won the battle. Tears come to my eyes and run quietly down my cheeks.

What if I never get over it? Will I lose my stars? What will become of The Yucca? My reputation? My life? Will I end up homeless under a bridge? Will my friends stand by me? Will they remain my friends if I am no longer good at anything in the kitchen? All of London will laugh at me, I have been a VIP for many years, the journalists will slaughter me.

My throat tightens. I sit on my bed, depressed.

※

In the evening I do not touch the meal brought by the kitchen helper. Yet I see that the Fendant sauce is on the menu, but I do not care. I am stunned by what I have discovered, that my health has failed me so quickly.

At bedtime with a shaky hand, I take too many pills, I know I should not, but I want to. I want to knock myself out, yet the pain tonight is bearable, but I do not want to think any more. I just want to sleep for a few hours and if possible, not have nightmares. I will not stand another restless night. When I think that before, only a few months ago, I used to fall asleep rapidly and wake up a few hours later ready to start a new exciting day. It seems like a long way off today given my miserable condition. Another life, which I bitterly regret.

CHAPTER 39

Last night I went to bed feeling low, but this morning I feel better, a bit stunned by the medication as I almost doubled the dose. A new sensation has invaded me. Maybe optimism? Or hope?

I dreamt about my precious grandmother. She looked so real that when I opened my eyes, for a few seconds, I thought she was in the room. I do not remember the dream precisely, but it seems to have brought some relief to my inner turmoil.

Before taking a shower, I look at the mirror and I hardly recognise myself. I have aged, a grey beard has grown, my hair is too long, in a mess, and not really clean. I have put on weight, with an unattractive pot belly showing. I have not moved for weeks, there's no miracle, I am starting to be flabby.

Far from avoiding my reflection in the mirror, I keep staring at myself to imbue my brain with what I do not want to see anymore.

In the shower I recall the serene impression left by my dream. I want to keep that serenity in mind. I remember now when my grandmother was telling me: "to deal with your enemies you have to know them well". Even though granny's enemy was usually a rebellious ingredient that did not suit her new recipe. Knowledge is the key to success and the key to get out of the most complex situations.

Having shaved and dressed in clean clothes, I slowly walk to my office with a cup of tea. I turn on my computer in order to consult the sites of my enemies: lumbago, mental health - clinical depression, meditation and yoga. To tell the truth, I know nothing about these subjects. So, I want to learn as much as possible to understand what I need to do to get out of this bad situation as quickly as possible. Attacking evil at its source.

Despite my reluctance to admit it, I noticed a deterioration of my mental health. Just the thought that this condition could last makes me shudder with horror. I hate those moments when I feel bad, weak and diminished. No matter how hard I try to be positive, nothing helps. Like my back pain, I did not see this psychological deterioration falling on me, it imposed itself and now I cannot fight it. So, I might as well accept it in order to tame the beast.

And of course, I must learn how meditation and yoga work, because I cannot let Gaston go.

I must therefore submit to his odious blackmail.

"Gaston, any news since you told him about your insane plan?".

"None".

"Has he not yelled on the phone?".

"No, he has not".

"Threatening e-mails?".

"None".

"Did he send his lawyer to fire you?".

"No".

"The cops?".

"No".

"?????".

"Benedict, I am scared to death. I was expecting a nuclear reaction, but nothing, his silence is killing me".

"He may have had a heart attack".

"Do not say that! I am already anxious enough. If his heart gave out, I would never forgive myself".

"I can assure you that such a hard heart does not give up so easily".

Having switched on my computer and waiting for the system to set up, I check that the printer is supplied with paper, so that I can print out as much information as possible. With a sigh of resignation my new informative crusade begins.

First enemy: lumbago.

Source internet: Lumbago is caused by a muscular contraction of the back muscles. These muscles, subjected to a brutal movement, will contract to contain the movement. This defence mechanism aims to protect the articular system which would otherwise risk exceeding its physiological amplitude. By contracting violently, the muscles will remain spasmed, contracted, and this tension will cause pain. At the same time, by contracting the dorsal muscles which are attached to the vertebrae will pull them in inclination and rotation (most often on the same side) and lock them in this bad position. Osteopathy remains the leading method for the treatment of lumbago.

The people most prone to this type of muscle pain are those who are not in very good physical shape or those who work in physical occupations.

Symptoms of lumbago: pain in the back, sometimes buttocks and legs.

The pain felt in the case of lumbago will be recent, following an effort, of muscular origin (with significant stiffness in the lower back), and intense. The muscular tension sometimes leads to compression of the sciatic nerve, in which case the pain radiates to the buttocks and sometimes to the legs.

It is essential to avoid the chronicity of any lumbar disease: adaptation of behaviour to effort (Back School), adaptation of the workplace, new bedding, physical activity.

Causes of lumbago: inadequate effort. In addition, there are psycho-emotional constraints.

Articles on lumbago do not seem to be lacking on the internet. As I read them, I grasp that what is happening to me is not exceptional. The nervous and psychological tensions of the last few years triggered my back pain.

And I am beginning to understand what the doctor meant when he talked about the necessary changes to be made in my life. I have been living this crazy life for too long. What my back has just made me understand is that somewhere deep down inside part of me is fed up with this stressful lifestyle. I am not 20 years old anymore. When I was a young chef, I only had one ambition; to succeed, to build my business, to get Michelin stars and to earn money. But I did not slow down once I reached my goals, on the contrary, I wanted to go higher and chase that damn third star.

I see a glimmer of hope in the darkness. I just understood an important point, first of all what is happening to me has a cause and secondly, indeed, if I change my way of life, I can get out of it. If I do not change anything, there is no doubt that my condition will continue. Do I have a choice? No.

Well, let's move on to the second enemy: clinical depression. I am ashamed to consult the internet for a mental problem, which is certainly widespread, but still a hard blow to my ego and my pride!

Clinical depression: source internet

Clinical depression can affect anyone. But "being down" does not mean "being depressed". When the illness strikes, it is associated with disorders, disabling feelings, which sometimes prevent you from living.

Distinguishing between clinical depression and depressed: "I am sad", "I am depressed". These expressions used over and over again do not make it possible to distinguish between ordinary clinical depression and real illness. Extending far beyond sadness, clinical depression is a disabling moral suffering, which disrupts relationships with family, friends and professional circles. It appears in the form of more or less long episodes. If it persists over time, it is called chronic clinical depression.

To speak of true clinical depression, in the medical sense of the term, several of the following symptoms must be felt for most of the day, for at least two weeks in a row:

- *Intense sadness, hypersensitivity;*
- *Decreased or lack of interest or pleasure;*
- *Eating disorders: loss of appetite and weight or, conversely, bulimia;*
- *Sleep disorders: insomnia or, on the contrary, a tendency to oversleep;*
- *Fatigue and loss of energy, even without any particular effort;*
- *Feelings of guilt or low self-esteem;*
- *Difficulty concentrating, intellectual slowing down;*
- *Dark thoughts or thoughts of death.*

In any case, it is difficult to establish one's own diagnosis. It is therefore preferable to consult your doctor.

Well, that reassures me! I feel a sense of relief. I am not suffering from clinical depression. I do have a few symptoms of being depressed, but the moments of weakness are usually followed by a rage to go back to work. I did not know that clinical depression is an illness. I thought it was a condition affecting weak people. What an uneducated person I have been!

So now, the third enemy: meditation.

Meditation: internet source.

The term meditation refers to a mental or spiritual practice. It often consists of an attention focused on a certain object of thought. For example, meditating on a philosophical principle in order to deepen its meaning or meditating on oneself with the aim of meditative practice in order to realise one's spiritual identity. Meditation generally implies that the practitioner brings his or her attention to a single point of reference.

Meditation is at the heart of the practice of Buddhism, Hinduism, Jainism, Sikhism, Taoism, Yoga, Islam, Christianity and other more recent forms of spirituality, but also medical. It is a practice aimed at producing inner peace, emptiness of mind, modified states of consciousness or progressive calming of the mind, or even simple relaxation, obtained by becoming familiar with an object of observation.

This text is followed by pages and pages of internet sites, especially on mindfulness meditation, which seems to have many followers all over the world. Everything I read is totally foreign to me. So meditating is all this? But how do you meditate? The sites describe the many benefits of meditation, but few describe how to practice it. I will have to explore this subject a little further. I thought it was just weird people who meditated, but I am surprised to discover that most heads of state practice meditation and that it is even taught in medical schools in Canada and in some universities around the world.

I am beginning to understand the change in Gaston. Meditation must undoubtedly help him at work to withstand the pressure. Whereas I have always kept everything inside, then exploded like a raging volcano. In fact, I have never stopped thinking, my brain has always been boiling. But from what I just read, meditation seems to bring peace to the brain, simply not thinking about anything for a few moments. Or letting thoughts pass by without holding on to them, without giving them more importance than what they are. I do not really understand what that means, but my instinct tells me that it must not be that easy to reach this level of non-action, or this level of acceptance, of consciousness.

Let's move on to the last and most annoying enemy: yoga.

Yoga: internet source.

Yoga is one of the six orthodox schools of Indian ästika philosophy. It has become in the West a discipline aiming, through meditation, moral asceticism and corporal exercises, to achieve the unification of the human being in its physical, psychic and spiritual aspects.

The four major traditional paths of yoga are jnana-yoga, bhakti-yoga, karma-yoga and raja-yoga. The term yoga is commonly used today to refer to hatah yoga, even though this discipline is only a branch of it. In 2014, the UN declared 21 June as International Yoga Day.

This is followed by all sorts of images about the different practices of yoga. My head is spinning from concentrating on the computer screen. I notice that there are pages and pages of websites on this subject. I cannot believe that there is so much interest in this discipline and even that the UN has recognised it and granted it one day a year. It would seem that the word yoga is used in all kinds of ways and that there is an incredible number of different practices and varieties of approaches. On the internet one finds all sorts of disciplines under the name yoga, the physical, the spiritual, the dynamic, even the mystical.

As my back starts to cause me serious pain again, my sitting position in front of the computer does not suit me for very long, I stop my research for today. I get up from my chair and try some exercises to relax the tension.

My discoveries have left me thinking.

Lumbago, that is what we are talking about! If I understand correctly, my bad posture, my damn temper and too much stress have caused my lumbago. I have also understood that this condition is not going to let go of me, can become chronic, if I do not make some changes in my life. Now I am thinking like a doctor! Am I becoming a fine psychologist? This idea is laughable.

I always wanted to have the last word, but in the end, it is my body that is having the last word. The expression "letting go" has not been part of my vocabulary, but now I have no choice but to let go.

I am less interested in what I read about meditation and yoga. To tell the truth, I have not understood much of it. Nothing seems very concrete or understandable. Unlike when you read a new recipe, which is very easy to understand, or when you read a financial balance sheet, the figures in black and white, it is concrete.

I pick up the pages of information I have printed from the internet. Walking slowly to the living room, I put the sheets on the table. I will read them later, for the moment my head is spinning. I need to lie down.

❋

"Hi Rick!".

"Hi Gaston, any news?".

"None".

"What do you mean, none?".

"Absolutely no reaction from Daniel".

"No volcanic explosion?".

"No".

"No yelling?".

"No".

"????".

"This silence is driving me nuts".

"In my opinion you are in a lot of trouble!".

*

After a nap, curled up on the sofa, I am concentrating so much on reading the printed sheets, that I do not hear the cleaning lady open the front door. Like last time she is very afraid to see me and screams with surprise.

I start to laugh. The situation is really funny. She is stunned by my reaction and remains on the threshold, unable to move or speak. She looks at me with a mixture of horror and fear, hesitating with which attitude to adopt. Then, her face relaxes. She smiles.

I think the hatchet is buried. To let her work in peace and having regained some strength, I pick up the printed sheets and go back to my office.

*

"Boris, I am freaking out!".

"What do you want to do?".

"I cannot stand this silence any longer. I have made him the silliest proposal and nothing, no reaction".

"You just have to wait, my dear Gaston, he is going to end up yelling, as usual".

"I am going to his flat, give me the keys of the van. I know that I am taking a huge risk, but I cannot stand his silence".

"You are suicidal!".

"I need to know what is going on. I am going there".

"What kind of wood do you wish for your coffin? Fir tree? Larch? Have you written down your will?".

"Do not start Boris, I am already tense enough".

The doorbell rings. The cleaning lady opens the door. I can hear voices exchanging greetings. It is a slightly pale Gaston who enters my flat. As he does not find me sprawled out on the sofa in the living room, as usual, I see his astonished look going around the place before seeing that I am in the office. He approaches very slowly and after the usual greetings, falls silent. His incredulous look shows that he just read what is on my computer screen. The site I am consulting is about meditation. On his face I see nothing but confusion and before he recovers from his surprise, mischievously, answering his silent question, I confirm that yes, I am inquiring about his proposal, that I am not so stubborn after all.

He looks so surprised that I wonder what image of a narrow-minded monster I have given him in the past. I ask him to talk to me about meditation, as I have difficulty in understanding how it works. I enthusiastically tell him about my morning's research and discoveries.

Total silence from Gaston. On his face is the expression of someone who has just seen a UFO.

To say the least, he did not expect my reaction at all. He seems so taken by surprise, which deep down inside is not to displease me, that he cannot utter a word.

So that he can gather his thoughts and as I also need one, I offer him a cup of tea. In my good mood, I also offer one to the cleaning lady, who, so surprised, drops her bucket of water on the floor. She looks at me frightened. I tell her it is nothing, that there are worse things in life.

From the way Gaston and the cleaning lady look at each other while I put the kettle on, I understand that they have never seen me being so nice and polite. But they do not know what it is like to endure so much pain, they do not know what a cruel life lesson I have just learned.

It is with small steps, a suspicious look on her face, that the cleaning lady approaches. Gaston has regained some senses. He grabs the jar of sugar, picks-up four cubes and puts them in his mug.

Having two visitors makes me very happy, even if they are rather stupefied. Has loneliness weighed more heavily on me than I am willing to admit?

The three of us sit around the table in my luxurious kitchen drinking an excellent tea. I have always made it a point of honour to order the best selection on the market.

To break the heavy silence, I dare to ask Gaston: "Where does this habit of putting so many cubes of sugar in your tea come from?".

"It comes from my childhood; my family was rather poor and sugar was non-existent. I grew up with the idea that sugar was a rare commodity, only for wealthy people. Today my life has taken a more pleasant financial turn, so I enjoy the fact that I can swallow as many sugar cubes as I want".

I am stunned by his answer. I know nothing about Gaston's childhood.

The cleaning lady then speaks in a slightly shy voice: "Sugar was also a rare commodity when I grew up, so I know exactly what you mean".

She speaks fluent English, at least once she is no longer frightened of me. But where does she come from? Her accent does not reveal much. I must have this information somewhere in my files.

Gaston comes to my rescue: "You have a slight accent; may I ask you where you come from?".

"From Kenya. Not from Nairobi, the capital, but from a small village in the middle of the countryside. She laughs nervously, adding that even if she told us the name of her birthplace, we would not know where it is as it is not indicated on the maps. She adds that she comes from the Luo tribe. However, she is willing to bet that the tea that the three of us are drinking right now comes from a leading Kenyan tea supplier, James Finlay Kenya, in Kericho county. Then she starts to describe its aroma, flavour and subtleties as if she were an expert".

She adds then: "James Finlay Kenya, is located in the highlands of Kericho at the heart of Kenya's tea growing region, west of the Great Rift Valley and bordering the Mau Forest. It covers 5,200 hectares of tea fields over nine gardens, and 1,200 hectares of preserved indigenous forest. At an elevation of approximately 6,500ft above sea level, Kericho's climate is comparatively cool and wet, while two rainy seasons during the year, in March-June and in October-December, ensure consistent growth".

I cannot help but look at her as if I am seeing her for the first time. Yet she has been working for me for years. She is a very competent employee and a tea specialist! I might not be at the end of my discoveries, now that I have opened my eyes and my heart to the outside world. The atmosphere in the kitchen suddenly relaxed, a simple question about sugar put everyone at ease. Unbelievable!

However, I remain pensive. I thought my childhood was devoid of financial resources, but some persons around me have probably experienced worse. Not even being able to afford sugar! What kind of childhood did these two have?

I find myself drinking my tea very slowly. Would I like to prolong this agreeable moment? My slowness does not escape Gaston, who, looking at his watch, sees that time is running out. He has left the tray of my meal in the living room and goes to fetch it back to the kitchen. The cleaning lady thanks me and goes back to work.

As Gaston begins to speak, I raise my hand to silence him and formally announce that I accept his deal: "I will submit to your plan, but you must promise to run the restaurant during my absence and that you will not accept any job offer from another restaurant. I am aware that with the additional work you will need support, therefore I give you carte blanche to hire the chef of your choice".

I also add that, as I said when he arrived, I spent the morning on the internet consulting sites on meditation and yoga and I did not understand much of it. Now I rely on him to enlighten me, in simple terms, as if he were talking to a child, because I need to understand before I start practising.

Gaston remains speechless.

Probably he did not expect such a quick and total victory. I take advantage of his surprise, and not having completely lost my mind, to tell him that I understand that in order to practice yoga one must not suffer from lumbago, so for the moment I propose to concentrate on meditation.

He looks completely lost and ironically asks: "Are you still the unbearable Daniel or a kind spirit has taken possession of his brain?".

I laugh nervously. He adds in a very serious voice: "First you offer me a cup of tea, which by the way has never happened since we have known each other, for years, then you accept my proposal without making a scene, without yelling, and on top of that you ask me for advice about meditation!".

In a very peaceful voice, I answer: "Yes, perhaps the monster has left my body and I am human again".

The ensuing silence is heavy, Gaston has lost his tongue. We stare at each other, then the cleaning lady somewhere in the flat starts singing in the language of her country. A joyful light melody that invades the rooms. This seems to unsettle Gaston even more, with round eyes full of surprise, he seems to have been propelled to another planet: "What is more, there is a Kenyan woman, a tea specialist, singing in your flat!".

I smile as I reply: "Yes!". Then I look him straight in the eye, bring my face closer to his and gently say: "Could you please ask her what her name is because I have not got a clue?".

We both burst out laughing. A liberating laughter that does not stop for long minutes, tears run down our cheeks.

I know now that the solution is within me, that I have to change my old ogre habits if I want to be healthy again. Being nice and polite is part of the change.

However, I did not imagine for a second that those around me would find it difficult to accept this new Daniel. I think it will take some time for them to understand that I am a monster who is perfectly acceptable.

Gaston does not even answer my question about meditation and hurries back to the restaurant. It is time to take command of The Yucca.

When the cleaning lady announces her departure, she notices that I have not touched the dish of food on the kitchen table and advises me to eat if I want to regain my strength. I reply with a smile that she sounds like my mother. She tells me she has six children and is used to dealing with recalcitrant kids who refuse to eat.

The door closes slowly behind her, I am stunned. I did not even flinch when she called me a recalcitrant kid. I was not aware that she was a mother of six, to tell the truth, before today I probably had not exchanged more than ten sentences with her. Six children! Do I pay her well enough? Living in London is expensive. I wonder if her file is not with Boris. I grab the phone.

It is in a very neutral voice that Boris answers: yes, I pay her well, even very well (at least I have not been a total moron) and no she does not live in London, just a bit outside, in a quiet village. If he is surprised by my questions, he does not show it. Even when I ask her name, he does not flinch: it is Faith. She is a widow with six kids aged between 19 and 5. He adds that she speaks English and Swahili. As if that could help me! I do not even know what Swahili is, what it sounds like, before today I had never even heard that word.

Gaston is in shock; he cannot manage to start the van. He remains paralyzed, his hands grabbing the wheel. His crazy plan has taken an unpredictable turn. He never for a second thought that his boss would inquire about his proposition, let alone accept it! Now what to do? What is the next step? Gaston feels trapped in a situation that he created, but which suddenly escapes him completely.

Well, he will have to avoid talking about yoga. How can he admit to his boss that he has never set foot in a class and that he does not even practice it? And he has to find out about meditation, because even if he does practice it, he cannot claim to be an expert, as he suggested.

He cannot wait to tell the good news to Rick, Boris and Benedict. No doubt they will find it hard to believe. And he is also happy that he no longer has to wear orange clothes, he cannot stand that colour.

In the next few weeks, he will have to work very hard. Since the clients fled the restaurant months ago, the finances are very low.

As he gets back on the road, he reflects that the Daniel he saw a few moments ago is a complete stranger.

Boris puts the handset slowly down. He wonders if he was dreaming.

When he saw Daniel's home number displayed, his heart started beating faster and anxiety overtook him. He had to make a superhuman effort not to panic.

But the conversation with a very calm Daniel destabilised him. To tell the truth, Boris had never heard Daniel speak so calmly and serenely, not to mention the fact that he was interested in his cleaning lady!

Tears come to Boris' eyes, it seems that Gaston's plan has worked!

The future looks suddenly brighter. He had considered leaving The Yucca. But now a huge challenge awaits them all if they want to save the restaurant. The finances are so bad that he wonders how he will be able to pay the bills at the end of next month if the customers do not come back.

CHAPTER 40

I wake up all twisted, aches and pains, as if I fought a boxing match all night long. This lumbago is definitely not going to let go of me any time soon.

I grab the box of medicines and after taking the required dose, I noticed that it is almost empty. The prescription is not renewable. I need to contact Dr Lloyd.

But first I have to go to the bathroom to make myself presentable. Those damn nightmares are starting to seriously ruin my nights, and my days for that matter. When I wake up in the morning, I do not remember enough to know what is going on in my subconscious. I have always believed that dreams and nightmares have a rational meaning. During sleep the brain relives known situations. But how do you identify which ones if you only have a diffused memory in the morning?

I sigh, not having an answer to this question.

After taking a shower, despite the medication already swallowed, the pain becomes unbearable. I call the doctor.

At the other end of the line, he is very cheerful and promises to come as soon as his schedule permits. This doctor is a real enigma to me, while everyone is reluctant to come to my flat, he seems to be delighted.

While waiting for his visit, I practice some physical exercises recommended by Damian. Only a few weeks ago

I would have found it perfectly ridiculous to be alone in my living room doing gymnastics. Today, I am happy to have the opportunity to take my mind off worries and I feel like I am doing something positive. What is more, it works, slowly as the exercise progresses, my back relaxes and the pain is reduced. But I am realistic, I still have a mountain to climb to regain my health.

When the doorbell rings, I hasten to open it, holding one hand on my hip so as not to upset that part of my body which has become very angry and unpredictable.

It is the doctor, all smiling and joking. He tells me, laughing, that every time he comes to see me, he meets my neighbours. These neighbours look at him as if he is going into a den of lions. My next-door neighbour, named Maxwell, even told him that if one day he needed help, all he had to do was shout, he would break down my door and beat me up!

I cannot utter a word. Once again, I feel ashamed of my attitude of the past. Dr Lloyd, probably sensing that I am uncomfortable with this subject, gets down to business.

"I am amazed that you are up and about, it is a good thing!".

"Follow me, you will understand".

In the office, I show him Damian's e-mail describing the physical exercises. Carefully reading the instructions, he nods: "I think they are very good". Then seeing the signature, he adds: "It would be a good thing to consider going to a Back School, but as soon as you have recovered, for the moment the pain is too acute".

"Gaston suggested meditation, I am interested to learn how".

I pretend to ignore his astonished face and show him the sites I have looked at on the internet, while humbly adding that I do not understand much. It takes him a few seconds to recover from the shock of this information. Coming to his senses he adds: "I have practised meditation for years. It has helped me, and still does, go through difficult moments, so I can only warmly recommend that you try it".

Then he asks me to lie down on my bed to examine me. Luckily, despite my pain this morning, he is not worried and renews the prescription.

I quickly get dressed and wanting to make amends for my past bad attitude towards him, I offer to drink a cup of tea. Like Gaston and Faith, the incomprehension can be seen on his face. Now it is official, there are all traumatized! And many more, I guess. I sigh at the prospect of having to drink a lot of cups of tea in the future, if I want to become a member of the respectable human race again.

I put the kettle on telling my visitor: "This tea is the best I could find on the market, it comes from Kenya according to Faith, my cleaning lady".

With disconcerting sincerity, he replies: "Stop, this is too much! That you want to practice meditation is already a shock, that you offer me a cup of tea is another shock, but on top of that you talk nicely about your housekeeper, that is a bit too much for my brain!".

He is right. I spent my time yelling at The Yucca's employees, at the suppliers, at the neighbours, at his colleague, at him too. The list goes on and on.

"I would like to know more about you. If you do not mind? If you are uncomfortable, I can drop the subject".

Having discovered the day before that Gaston and Faith came from more modest families than mine, I feel a new curiosity growing in me to know in which environment the persons around me come from so that I can better understand them.

Dr Lloyd's background comes as a surprise. He is the heir to a noble and reputedly extremely wealthy family. His father is a well-known figure of the City of London high finance. I am very surprised to hear that. I would never have guessed that Dr Lloyd, wearing old faded jeans and an everlasting white T-shirt, came from such wealth and I ask him why he did not want to follow in his father's footsteps to make a very good living.

I hand him the mug of tea and the sugar bowl. I cannot help observing how many cubes Dr Lloyd is going to add to his drink. He sweeps away my offer of sugar with his hand: "I never take sugar in my tea".

Then he explains: "High finance does not suit me. I do not like to crush people with power. Money deep down does not bring happiness, even if it makes life much easier. I have always wanted to help others. Having been brought up in a very closed and privileged environment, I am only interested in simple, normal people. My dream is to work in the humanitarian field. One day I hope to go to Africa".

"So come and chat with Faith one day if you want to learn more about Kenya, where she comes from".

He looks at me, his eyes full of surprise, then after a moment's reflection, answers: "Why not".

Suddenly remembering what Faith told me the day before, I add: "She is not from the capital Nairobi, but from a small village deep in the bush, which is not even mentioned on the maps".

All intrigued by what I have just discovered about him, I dare to ask: "I am surprised that you seemed always at ease with me and this from the start, despite the fact that I did not give you a good welcome and treated you even worse".

A little hesitant, he goes on telling me that this is due to the relationship with his tyrannical father, who is not kind to him, the last boy of the family. His father finds him too different from the other heirs. His brothers were already accomplished sportsmen as children, tough guys. Unlike him, who was frail and sensitive, in poor health and interested in art and culture, who spoke willingly with the household staff, as well as with the inhabitants of the neighbourhood. "My father is an extremely cold person. He was intolerant when we were growing up, and still is today, to anybody he considers weak" he adds with a sigh. Divorce between father and son was consummated long before he came of age. Since he left the family's nest, he rarely sees his father, occasionally on the streets of London.

However, he regularly dines with his mother in a small restaurant in central London. Relations with his brothers are almost non-existent. He modestly says that as a child and teenager he suffered a lot, he felt rejected by them. But today, he adds, he uses this experience with his patients. He knows how to recognise the real tough guys compared to the fake tough guys. He adds with a wink of laughter that he knew at first glance that I was a fake tough guy and that I had the capacity within me to change, to become a better person. Also, he was curious to meet me, like many others he had seen my picture in the medias. He wanted to meet a celebrity who had nothing to do with finance. Then he asks me where is the sculptural blonde who accompanied me to VIP parties in recent months.

I am taken aback; I do not know what to say. I have the impression that this doctor knows more about me than I do! To avoid the discussion getting bogged down in sentimentality, I laugh a little nervously: "The sculptural blonde, Lilly, has left me".

I add: "She works in a bank in the City".

"She did not deserve you".

I do not comment, I am not so sure.

CHAPTER 41

Summer is coming to an end. I spent the last few months cooped up inside my flat watching the outside world from my window, as if I no longer belonged to the human race. Resigned, I gave up fighting. The disease has won. I let go and accepted my new situation.

No more social life, no more parties, no more invitations, no more work, no more flattery, no more golf, total emptiness. It is as if the rest of the world has forgotten me. And I think I have forgotten the rest of the world.

The pain has subsided, but I still think about it with shivers of horror, fearing that it might sneakily come back, too aware of what awaits me in the hours that follow. Having so much pain traumatised me.

After the initial revolt, I resigned myself to accept living at a very slow pace. I do not know how I came to accept my condition. To tell the truth, I am sometimes surprised that I have come to terms with it. I gave up fighting. Today I only have one wish: to get better. I am not even asking for full recovery, I just want to be able to go to work, to live a normal life without extravagances. I am ready to make compromises, I am ready to go to church, do sports, and I do not know what else, to be healthy again. I still worry every day at the thought of staying in this state of disrepair.

Since I accepted my fate, my body started to relax and improvements appeared, slowly but surely. And I had to accept the tears. They began to flow one day, when I was just watching a silly film on television. I did not understand why, but I did not put up any resistance. Sometimes I have to take refuge in my bathroom, when Faith is present, so as not to show the flood and to keep my dignity. I have to admit that since I gave myself the right to cry, I feel better.

※

Rick, Florian, Jake and Michael met regularly during the summer. Knowing full well that Daniel would not be able to join them, they preferred not to tell him about their encounters.

They are all terrified about Daniel's collapse. A misadventure that could well happen to them, especially Michael who suffers from PTSD (Post Traumatic Stress Disorder) due to the fiasco of his former restaurant "Le Coralie". He was clumsy with Daniel and feels guilty. He is aware that he has not been able to find the right words and has not acted appropriately with his long-time friend.

They felt helpless and lost seeing Daniel's descent into hell. Their only hope seems to be that their friend has seriously accepted his fate and according to Damian, who is an expert, this is the only way to get back on track. Damian, who was and still is a precious ally, willingly answering the questions of the chefs and reassuring each of them that everything is going to be all right, it just takes time, a good awareness and of course you have to change your habits.

Without Daniel's knowledge, they did not want to worry him, they regularly visited Gaston and Benedict at The

Yucca. They gave precious advice on how to run the business and even spent a few evenings working there to lead the team, left without a captain. To be frank The Yucca was on the verge of sinking, which was what Gaston, Benedict, Boris and Rick had realised when they started to meet incognito to discuss the situation. Daniel saw nothing, too lost in his quest for the stars, he had not even noticed that the bookings were dropping. The third Michelin star he was so much hoping for was a utopia under his impossible management. Keeping the first two was also difficult with a boss yelling all the time and scaring off the employees. And Daniel had made too many enemies, notably the customers he had ended up refusing, the gossip spread by Marine and the revenge of some dismissed employees, like Viviane. Ah that one! She took a nasty revenge, talking ill about Daniel at parties gathering journalists and important clients.

It goes without saying that all the women that Daniel rejected or mistreated enjoyed the fall of The Yucca's chef. Only Lilly refrained from commenting.

CHAPTER 42

London's gardens turn into beautiful autumn colours. Apart from a few walks to the pharmacy, the local hairdresser, or just to stretch my legs in the nearby park, I do not get much out of my flat.

My friends regularly keep in touch, especially Jake, who comes home between filming his new TV shows. Each time he brings a bottle of Cornalin which I enjoy so much. Dr Lloyd knows nothing about this little arrangement between Jake and me. He still forbids me to drink alcohol, despite my timid attempts to convince him that it would be good for my morale. After Jake leaves, I stash the bottle in a place where Dr Lloyd cannot see it. He is smart. I think he knows me well.

My days are now timed like a Swiss clock. Waking up often with back pain. Drinking tea from Kenya provided by Faith. Then slowly dragging my feet to the bathroom. Naked as a worm back in my bedroom to dress myself in an oversized tracksuit. I have not worn shirts in months, let alone ties. Then, breakfast in the kitchen, not forgetting to take my dose of medication after eating in order not to upset my stomach. In the past I rarely took medication, sometimes for a headache. Now I feel like I have become an addict, I cannot do without it. I know that one day I will have to reduce the dose, but for the moment I cannot. Fortunately, the injections were no longer necessary.

Every day, like a ritual, I grab the box of medicines and swallow the tablets. Not a morning goes by when I do not wonder, alone in my kitchen, how I got to this point. How in such a short time I transformed myself from a hyperactive man to this nothing, dragging myself painfully from one room to the other, being alert to the slightest false movement that could upset my inner enemy.

After all these "Why? Why me?" that never led to anything, the morning is spent in front of my computer to keep in touch with the outside world, followed by lunch in the kitchen, always delivered by a more or less terrified kitchen helper.

Dr Lloyd having given me the green light to do the exercises recommended by Damian, I practise them every day. Then follows a long wait in the afternoon, eagerly waiting for visits, or calls, before the evening meal arrives, then off to bed very early, hoping with anxiety that I will not move around too much in my sleep to avoid these damn pains.

And if I managed to avoid the very dreaded yoga classes, Gaston must have forgotten about them he is too busy I guess, I learned how to meditate. Yes, I, the Chef Daniel, I meditate. Oh, it was not easy, I had to consult dozens of websites, read some books lent by Gaston before I understood how to do it. My brain, which complicates everything, took a while to understand that in fact meditating is very simple.

Since then, I have practised every day and I greatly appreciate these windows of freedom, of calm in my head, these moments of deep awareness. It has become vital.

CHAPTER 43

Second week of November, the first snow of the season fell on London, well in advance this year. I discovered it this morning with surprise when I opened the curtains, very thin, but it will hold as the cold is biting. From the window of my sleeping room, I look at the people in the street walking carefully, in order not to fall, and cars moving very slowly. Employees docilely on their way to work. I envy them being able to live a normal life. I would love to stretch my legs, but I do not dare to go outside for fear of falling.

Significant improvements of my health appeared this autumn. I am much more mobile and the pain is less severe. But the problem is that at the slightest false movement I feel like I am pierced by a sword, a sharp pain knocks me down and takes my breath away. On the other hand, it does not last as long as before, which is a relief.

My problem is no longer just mechanical, but also psychological. Dr Lloyd knows it and I know it. But I do not want to talk about it. I do not have the strength to consult a shrink. Misplaced pride, I suppose.

It is very surprising to everyone, and to myself, that I learnt to completely trust Dr Lloyd and only want to be treated by him. He has kindly resigned himself to my wish and visits me regularly, apparently with a certain pleasure which I do not think is fake. He renews my prescription, after examining me and asking me lots of questions, his forehead wrinkled by the seriousness of the moment, always the same questions by the way and my answers are always the same. Dr Lloyd is conscientious. Then we drink tea, eat biscuits baked by Faith and talk about anything and everything.

My life has changed a lot, to say the least, and above all, I have changed a lot. I no longer raise my voice, nor yell, nor show signs of impatience, no more sarcasm, nor unpleasant words. Today my housekeeper, Faith, comes into my flat with a smile on her face and we spend a lot of time chatting in the kitchen. I have learnt tons of things about her life, about Kenya, which I intend to visit one day. I asked her if she would be willing to do more work at my flat, as I really need help and enjoy her company. She now comes four times a week. She does my shopping and takes care of everything else. Of course, I raised her salary, I even asked Boris to triple it. I feel a new sense of well-being when I please the people around me. Faith was in shock when she discovered her new wage, could not believe it and then thanked me with tears in her eyes. Just seeing her so happy, made me want to shed a tear too. I no longer consider her an employee, almost a friend.

The week after that scene, she appeared one day with her arms full of bags, flanked by one of her sons, Oliver, a muscular young man. Then she told me that in her youth she worked at the Carnivore, a well-known restaurant chain in Kenya. She started cooking with Oliver at her side. Nobody before would have dared to cook for me. I was a bit stunned at first, then I smiled, I was just happy that someone finally took the initiative to do it. And I was curious.

To see them both in my kitchen, perfectly at ease, it is obvious they are used to working together, filled me with a feeling of serenity. Then the moment of the verdict arrived. The appetizing plate in front of me, the two faces of Faith and Oliver anxious as I stuck the fork into the dish and then brought the food to my mouth. The dish was delicious. I was impressed and showered them with compliments, to their delight. Then we had a great time eating and laughing together.

That was the day Oliver was hired to work at The Yucca. During our discussion I learned that he had just come out of a cooking course and was looking for a job. No doubt this was the hidden agenda behind Faith's initiative. I found this funny and as he had just proved that he was very promising, I hired him on the spot, called Boris and Gaston to inform them. That same evening Oliver started his job at The Yucca. Since then, he has worked hard, has excellent relations with his colleagues, especially the new chef that Gaston hired, Elliot, whom I find curious and gifted.

No doubt to the great relief of the kitchen helpers, Elliot volunteered to bring my meals every day. He always takes advantage of this time alone with me to ask about particular recipes. A few months ago, his questioning would have made me mad, but today I am flattered that a motivated young chef asks so many questions. I feel I am a reference and this is not to displease my ego which has wavered but, let's be honest, is still there somewhere.

In just a few weeks Gaston has taken up the challenge of managing The Yucca with a lot of effort, energy and hours of hard labour. I wonder how he does it. "No more yoga classes during the day!", I sometimes tell him joking. Gaston always evades my references to yoga; I do not really know why. Today he has dark circles around his eyes, has lost weight and is under a lot of stress. Fortunately, he can count on Benedict and Boris to do their utmost to help him.

I think he better understands the pressure I was under in the first few years after the opening of The Yucca and had to make my place in the cruel competition of London's culinary establishments, not to mention the financial worries. Gaston now understands how I became the filthy character I was until a few months ago. And through the experience that Gaston is having right now, which I am observing closely, I am beginning to understand better what happened in my life to become this, shall we say, difficult, even downright obnoxious person.

Gaston is suffering, but learns quickly. I have full confidence in him, he consults me for everything, even for details. I always give him carte blanche, but I think that today consulting me has become a pretext to visit me and chat a little "between chefs". I have become his confidant. In any case he can count on my unfailing support, I have always appreciated Gaston and to see him today at the head of The Yucca fills me with pride. Of course, I am still the boss, the owner, but I can no longer be physically present. I even decided to waive part of my salary.

Gaston was very surprised when I announced this decision. Very seriously, he told me that he did not think many starred chefs would be humble enough to do so. To tell the truth, I surprised myself by accepting this idea that came to my mind one fine morning over breakfast, and I am even more surprised to see how well I came to terms with it.

Gaston is disappointed with some employees he thought he could trust. He might have to fire one or two who do not respect his authority. Once he lost his temper and began shouting at them. He looked down when he told me so. However, he is impressed by Elliot and Oliver. They seem to make a good team. I smile as I recall my first encounter with Elliot. Gaston had brought him to the flat before his recruitment so that I could give my opinion. Elliot was a little intimidated and embarrassed to be in front of the boss.

Later, before the front door closed, I heard Elliot tell Gaston: "He does not deserve his reputation as a bad guy".

I just had time to hear Gaston's response: "You did not know him before; he was a monster".

CHAPTER 44

Florian and Rick call on a regular basis to check up on me. Due to my condition and the geographical distances, we have not seen each other for months. They tell me what is happening in their lives and keep me posted about work. They even ask for advice when they have a problem.

They told me that they had noticed a profound change in me. I put my pride aside and explained to them frankly all the difficulties I had gone through. They listened carefully.

This was not seen as a weakness, but as a strength, as Florian told me: "It is courageous for a man to speak so frankly about how he feels". I did not know Florian was such a fine psychologist. It was against myself, against my deep-rooted ideas of being a superman that I had to fight the most.

Early December Michael left for China. The decision was made within a week. He and his wife, not having been able to forget their wonderful stay, accepted the offer from the management of the Shanghai Meridien to work there for 10 months. Before their departure, they came to see me. As I can no longer play golf, they brought a cake in the shape of a golf course. It was beautiful and delicious.

I found myself not blaming Michael for his reaction a few months ago when he hung up the phone on me. Moreover, Michael's attitude during this phone call was the basis of a salutary reflection, a questioning, an opening towards my friends. I hope Michael one day sees that his past trauma may blow up in his face. I wish my friend would take better care of himself, but I do not know how to tell him. Surprisingly, he emails regularly from Shanghai. I believe he is homesick. He misses our evenings at Jake's. I understand him. I am not in China, but I cannot go to Jake's place anymore. I feel as much in exile as Michael does.

Since I spend most of my time at home, I see things differently, I see life differently, I see the reactions of the people around me differently. I see my life differently.

I have not even thought much about Marine. I believe I am cured. I recently saw a picture of her in a cooking magazine, I almost did not recognise her. Of course, it was Marine, but the fascination is gone. To be honest, the pic was of someone who was not very nice. We had a great relationship, as far as I am concerned, but I have moved on. Yet I have no woman in my life, it is no wonder as I do not go out, and I am still ashamed of what I have learned about Lilly.

One day Gaston confessed he had noticed that Jules, the well-known journalist who regularly dined at The Yucca, was no longer among the guests. Being intrigued, he investigated with the help of Elliot whom we found out is a hobby hacker. It came as a huge surprise that Jules and Lilly are siblings! On top of that, Elliot found a photo of the famous Michelin critic; Mr Tornado. Contrary to the rumour that he is 35 years old, it is in fact a man in his seventies who smiles in front of the camera, beside him on the photo are his two children, Jules and Lilly!

As this is explosive information, we made Elliot swear never to reveal it to anyone. If this leaks and Mr Tornado learns that it came from us, The Yucca will be stripped of all its stars. Elliot's answer was astonishing: "No problem, I am used to sensitive information. For fun, I regularly hack the systems of banks, of newspapers, of government offices". We cut him off not wanting to hear more.

Thinking about Lilly I wonder how could I have been so selfish and not even had the curiosity during our relationship to inquire about her family? I recalled that she never mentioned them, now I know why.

On the business side, I hope that her father, Mr Tornado, does not hold a grudge against me if she tells him one day about the way I treated her. As Lilly and I appeared regularly in the media when we went out to parties, he must have been aware of our relationship. Maybe that is why he never came to The Yucca; he was waiting to see where our relationship was going. Or maybe he did not want to be accused of favouring a restaurant because the owner was his daughter's partner. In any case, I realise today that there was almost no way to receive the so wanted third star.

What is more, I found myself thinking tenderly of her during those months of solitude, but I did not dare to call her. I behaved too badly; I am too ashamed. Today I know that this woman is worth a million, she is kind, gentle, caring, intelligent, I could go on and on. I hope she is happy. I was such a jerk. I wish her to be in love, to have met someone better than me, which should not be too difficult.

CHAPTER 45

Snow is heavily falling on the capital, soothed by this immaculate white coat. Sitting in the living room, Gaston is preoccupied and nervous. He responds succinctly to my requests and avoids my gaze. After a few minutes of small talk, I cannot stand this attitude anymore and ask him frankly: "Is there a problem at The Yucca? Is it serious?".

Gaston takes a deep breath and reassures me: "No, there is no problem at the restaurant, everything is fine. But given our good relationship, I want to lighten my conscience, because I have not been terribly honest with you on one specific matter".

He does not know how to broach the subject, he hesitates. Then follows a short speech about the fact that he does not feel proud, that he has not acted elegantly, etc.

I do not see where this discussion is going and, intrigued, urge him to speak frankly. I have not seen Gaston so disturbed since I told him I had accepted his plan. He swallows, sweats, but eventually takes a deep breath and begins to tell me about an event from the past, saying that he hopes I will not get angry, that this will not change anything in our excellent relationship.

I am more and more perplexed and I am all ears. At the end of his speech, after a silence during which I digest what he has just told me, far from being offended, I start to laugh.

My God, Gaston, really fooled me!

His face relaxes. In fact, I did not know it at all, he just told me, but he had started a love affair with the famous Viviane. After a few weeks, he could not stand her anymore and did not know how to end this relationship. Viviane did not seem to want to give up on him. He had even nicknamed her "the other problem".

He had manipulated Viviane by telling her that I would greatly appreciate it if one of my employees dared to stand up to me and contradict me during the briefings, knowing full well that I was going to blow a fuse confronted with this rebellious attitude.

It happened exactly as Gaston had planned, I could not stand her and fired Viviane, solving Gaston's "other problem".

❄

After Gaston's departure, I reflect on what has just been said. I laid Viviane off, being manipulated by her lover who wanted to get rid of her.

I wonder how many people took advantage of my level of exhaustion to manipulate me? How many people told me nonsense that I swallowed without questioning the whole thing? How many times have I acted like a robot, taking for truth what I had just been told? How many times have I been fooled?

I would rather not know.

I was simply too tired to see further than the tip of my nose, my neurons did not work anymore.

CHAPTER 46

Today is a beautiful sunny day. What a joy to be able to walk down the street, even though my step is uncertain and I move slowly! What a joy to be among human beings, to breathe fresh winter air! The sun on my face fills me with energy. My spirits are so high that I almost feel like whistling.

To avoid being jostled by passers-by I bought a cane as recommended by Dr Lloyd. My pride put aside from being seen diminished, the cane gives me a reassuring stability.

Coming back from the drugstore situated around the corner, I am in a very good mood. I always make it a point of honour to be friendly with the employees, enjoying this interlude away from my flat. And, let's be honest, I am happy to have new boxes of my precious painkillers. Fearing to stumble, I stare at the icy ground strewn with leaves in front of me. I am afraid of falling, which would really upset my back.

A shadow blocks my path. I raise my head.

He is standing in front of me, his legs a little apart, slim figure, curly blond hair, just like in my memories of the competition. Toby! As if I could forget the one I nicknamed "the half-Swiss", given his origins.

He stares at me with very little kindness in his eyes: "So how is the great and unbearable Chef Daniel?".

He seriously annoys me, disturbs my beautiful walk, and on top of that he is provoking me.

One has to face life's problems.

I stand in front of him so close that my nose could touch his. Looking him straight in the eye, I calmly ask him in a controlled voice what his problem is. As he is a little shorter than me, I lower my head and as my body is much larger than his, I feel imposing.

He takes a step back and clears his throat. Then he pulls himself together: "I bet you do not recall where we met?".

"On the contrary, I know exactly who you are,", I reply, still annoyed at being disturbed. "You worked at The Yucca as a kitchen helper. I fired you".

And there he bursts out laughing nervously telling me what a nightmare it was to work under my orders with his friend Marcel, the famous chef who made me swallow awful dishes a few months ago on my way back from Scotland. Toby informs me somewhat arrogantly that he had great pleasure in stealing the junior chef Euan whom I had recruited to replace Viviane.

His speech over, he looks at me with a triumphant look on his face.

A silence settles in.

Then, in a very calm and relaxed voice, I reply: "Is that all I taught you?".

This seems to unsettle him; he looks at me a little disconcerted. He certainly did not expect this calm response. I have changed, but he does not know that, not yet.

"Yes, that is a question, is that all I have taught you?".

Visibly more and more destabilised, he does not answer. He seems to have suddenly lost his self-confidence.

"Did not I teach you anything other than good cooking, how about excellent cooking? Have I taught you to take revenge by making your former boss swallow filthy dishes? Did I teach you to steal other chefs' employees? Did I not teach you to work hard, to start all over again until you reached perfection? Did not I teach you to be disciplined, to always try to achieve excellence, to give the best of yourself and to be proud of it? Is that all I taught you, to look sarcastic and make fun of sick people?".

He seems to be stunned.

"What have you done with your life? By the way, I recall you are half Swiss, Swiss-German?".

"Yes, I am half-Swiss, but French-speaking, my mother comes from the South, Valais".

"Valais, home of the Cornalin! I hope you put this delicious wine on your card? You speak fluent French. But when I saw you a few weeks ago at the competition, you were talking on the phone in an incomprehensible dialect, I thought it was Swiss-German".

"Oh that! It was a language that I invented on the spot just to annoy you. When we were working together, I noticed that you could not bear not to control everything. And no, I did not think of adding a Cornalin to my wine list". He lets his voice linger and avoids my gaze.

"I hope that you completed your training in Switzerland or in France as you speak the language".

A tiny, barely audible and unglamorous "No" crosses his lips.

"You speak two languages fluently; you have an advantage over all of us and you did not take that advantage? Do you know what British chefs had to endure in terms of language difficulties when working abroad? What about your menu, does it at least contain dishes influenced by Swiss cuisine? Chocolate desserts?".

"No".

"Do you know that some of the best chefs are of Indian, Thai, Danish or other origins and provide a cuisine that makes my jaw drop? Do not you know that diversity comes from different cultures and influences? I ask you again, what have you done with your life?".

An awkward silence follows. Pale, he staggers on his legs, steps back. No doubt he did not expect this attitude from me. Then he regains his composure.

"You did not go abroad for your training either!".

"You did not need to make the same mistake".

He lowers his eyes, like a kid caught in the act of doing something stupid. I believe I have put my finger on something he had not thought of.

I clear my voice and apologise for the past. I should not have fired him, he was promising. On the other hand, Marcel, I shake my head.... That was another story, he simply did not have it in him to be a good chef. But he, Toby, it was his attitude that disappointed me, he was influenced by Marcel who was pulling him down.

"I did not know you thought I was good", he says shyly and very surprised.

"That is why I was kicking your butt all day long, so that you would excel yourself. But no, all you could think of was fooling around with Marcel! I did not have time to lose, I had to keep the restaurant running at its highest level".

Of course, I do not admit that at that time I was heartbroken from losing Marine and that I had used them as scapegoats.

Then he says: "I heard what Marcel did to you and I was appalled. We do not have much contact these days, I kind of avoid him. You know Euan, the chef I stole from you a few months ago, he was not that good. He had an excellent training, but he lacked imagination. He stole some recipes from me and went to work elsewhere. He betrayed me. I had given him responsibilities, paid him a very good salary. In short, if it is any consolation, I was fooled".

"Welcome to my world! And no, that does not please me. Some people just cannot be trusted".

"You do not have too bad an opinion of me then?".

"Apart from the fact that you have unfortunately not taken advantage of your skills, no, I do not have a bad opinion of you", I add with a smile. "But please put a Cornalin on your wine list, it is my favourite red wine, I might even visit you one day".

He laughs a little. Then he holds out his hand.

"No hard feelings then?".

"No hard feelings", I say, shaking his hand and smiling.

CHAPTER 47

"May I help you?".

I thought I was alone in the entrance of the building where my flat is situated. I turn around slowly to face my interlocutor. After my encounter with Toby, I am all smiles, but my smile disappears in a split second. My face freezes and my jaw drops.

My next-door neighbour is standing in front of me.

He is imposing, muscular, immense, all tanned, hair held back in a ponytail, diamond shaped earrings on both ears. The same neighbour who sent threatening registered letters concerning night-time disturbance, due to me listening to booming music. His flat is situated next to mine. He even called the cops several times. I have made a point of carefully avoiding this neighbour since Dr Lloyd told me that he wanted to beat me up.

But what is he doing here in the morning? He is usually never home in the morning! I have spied on his comings and goings to know exactly what his schedule is in order to avoid him at all costs. The months have passed, I have not listened to classical music. I noticed how little soundproofed the walls are. When I hear that my neighbour is in his flat, I turn off the television for fear of making him angry.

Facing him, and his huge size, I feel even more diminished with my cane in one hand. I have just dropped on the floor the bag of medicines. In my condition, bending down to pick something up is quite an adventure.

My neighbour slowly approaches me.

I start to sweat. His face a few centimetres from mine, suddenly he bends down, picks up the bag and gives it to me.

I almost let go of that damn bag again. He presses the lift button, so I have no choice but to go up with him. The moment is embarrassing. I watch him from the corner of my eye. The guy is just a bundle of muscles, a huge bundle of muscles! He must be about 6'6 and quite a few pounds heavier than me. In the small lift he takes up all the space. I feel as imposing as a sparrow.

But my neighbour looks comfortable, despite the palpable tension. He even makes conversation, who knows why.

"By the way, my name is Maxwell".

"Nice to meet you, I am Daniel".

"Lloyd and Faith told me that you are a nice guy who lost his mind over work".

Ah, they talk about me, how embarrassing! I had no idea, but it is logical, they must cross paths frequently in the corridors of the building.

He adds that once he also suffered from burnout because of work, but now he is ok.

He is in no hurry once we reached the third floor where our flats are situated. I would give a lot to be safe at home. But I do not dare to rush.

I pull myself together, gather my courage: "I am sorry about the music, I didn't know that the walls were so poorly soundproofed".

"What kind of music do you listen to? From my apartment it sounds awful".

"Uh, it is Vivaldi".

"Viva what?".

"Vivaldi. He is an Italian composer. But since I realised it was a nuisance, I do not listen to music anymore", I hastily add. I cannot get it out of my head that this bundle of muscles told Dr Lloyd in the past that he wanted to beat me up and now that I see the man's stature, I am keeping a very low profile. I do not want to provoke him.

"Are you a chef?".

"Yes, I am the starred chef of The Yucca in Brixton".

"Never heard of it. I attach great importance to food; I do a lot of sport you see".

That I suspected.

"Is it your job, uh, sport?".

"No, I work in fashion, I am a designer of men's clothing".

God, he looks more like a truck driver! But when you think about it, bodybuilders also need clothes, even if it is thongs. Who knows, maybe he is a thongs designer? Carefully I keep my thoughts to myself.

We say goodbye. Once in my flat, I lean against the front door and let out a long sigh of relief. Sweat flows from my forehead.

And then the doorbell rings.

Like in a horror film, I open it slowly.

My neighbour stands in front of me. He hands me something that I do not immediately identify. I take it mechanically.

"OK, you are in pain and the walls are thin, but as I am also a music lover, you must not stop listening to music, even your Italian spaghetti thing. But please use headphones".

He returns to his flat. I stand a few minutes on the doorstep, headphones in hand, too shocked to react.

CHAPTER 48

Today Gaston picked me up at my flat, in fact he dragged me to The Yucca. Somehow, I am ashamed of my condition. I am far from the man my employees used to see and I did not want to show them the pathetic, sick, diminished, aged chef I have become, walking with a cane.

But Gaston did not leave me much choice. Flanked by Benedict, not very talkative as usual, he made me get in his car and here I am at the scene of my crimes.

At first glance I notice that my Yucca trees are still in place, no Buddha statues, phew! The employees avoid me, some of them are frankly hostile, but the atmosphere is rather relaxed and some, to my great surprise, look sorry to see me in this state.

It is with pride and enthusiasm that Gaston and Benedict show me the new menu. After studying it closely, I give them my approval. During the silence that preceded my verdict, they held their breath, their faces tense.

Boris tells me about the financial situation. How can my establishment, which was doing so well, end up in the red? No need to be a genius to understand that many regular customers have fled The Yucca under my very bad management. Fortunately, there is hope as the bookings have resumed, slowly but surely, and with a new clientele.

Then Elliot shows me the new computer system he put in place. I am impressed, everything looks so easy and is password protected. I warmly congratulate him.

I think about my old computer at home and ask him if he could come by when he has a moment to have a look at it. My printer is not working very well and my internet connection is very slow. He accepts with pleasure and promises to come by soon, which surprises the employees who are within earshot.

If Elliot and Oliver, the newcomers, are very comfortable in my presence, they have never worked under my management, the others look simply traumatised. They are clearly ill at ease.

Once again, I am ashamed of my attitude of the past. Never before this visit to The Yucca have I been so confronted with the monster I was. It will take time before my employees understand that I have truly and sincerely changed, at least those who have not yet resigned. Boris has informed me that most of them will be leaving soon, no longer wishing to work with me.

In the car driven by Gaston on our way back to my place, I am pensive while watching the streets go by. Gaston, probably feeling that I need this moment to myself, does not break the silence.

Back at home, I confide in him. I tell him that I understand why he took me to The Yucca. On one hand so that I can understand what a monster I have been in the past with the staff and on the other hand so that I can see with my own eyes the excellent work done by himself and Benedict.

Gaston would like me to consider returning to work. By bringing me back to the scene of my crimes, he hoped that I would realise how much I love my restaurant and how much I have missed it in recent months.

He is somehow right, I take in how much I love The Yucca, but he is very wrong about one thing. I have no desire to go back to work if I am not 100% fit. Moreover, I saw that the establishment is doing well and this has completely reassured me. And I have to admit that given the catastrophic financial figures of the last few months under my management it is better that I let myself be forgotten for a while. I think the solution is that I should disappear so that the new clientele and the new employees can get used to Gaston.

The decision is made in a minute. I am going to go to the health centre run by Damian to finish my convalescence and follow his rehabilitation programme. This idea has been on my mind for a while.

It is not the reaction Gaston was hoping for, but he respects it.

After Gaston's departure, I pick up the phone and call Damian to book my stay. He informs me that a room will be available in two weeks' time, just before Christmas. I will not come back to London before I am healthy again. I promise myself.

I give Damian carte blanche to organise the necessary appointments. I intend to submit to whatever is advised or imposed upon me, even if I am a little anxious about the physical exercises and osteopathy is not my cup of tea.

Then I call Dr Lloyd who is delighted with my decision. He had been hoping for a while that I would come to this conclusion. He is going to bring me my medical file so that I can pass it on to the doctor at the centre.

I am going into a kind of exile to make the world forget who I was and to try to forget the monster I have been for years.

CHAPTER 49

I will be leaving for Stourpaine in two days. I am hugely motivated; I cannot stand these four walls any longer. I have already taken the suitcases out.

But how should you dress in a health centre? Lost in this dilemma, I call Rick. He burst out laughing, then gives me a few tips, adding that he is happy that I took the decision to go to this brother's health centre, he will see me more often. This means a lot to me. Here is one who, despite the fact that I did not always treat him well in the past, has remained faithful to me.

✳

Dr Lloyd is visiting me tonight, no worn jeans, no white T-shirt. He is smartly dressed. The suit and tie are blue and the shoes glow in the light. He will be having dinner at The Yucca. I am surprised to notice that he is terribly nervous. Answering my question, he admits that he is not used to eating in luxurious places since he left his wealthy family. I reassure him that he will feel very comfortable. But even this statement does not seem to calm his nervousness. He makes me laugh, in spite of himself.

To accompany him, I invited Faith. I thought it would be an excellent opportunity for these two to talk about Africa and Kenya, as Dr Lloyd mentioned his desire to learn more about this continent.

When Faith arrives dressed in a dashingly beautiful gorgeous red dress, our jaw drops just looking at her. She is not at all impressed to eat in one of London's top restaurants. However, I suspect that her offspring, Oliver, who works in the kitchen, better not do anything stupid tonight! The mother's verdict will be terrible.

They both leave me, taken to The Yucca by the restaurant's limousine. Elliot having brought my evening meal; I find myself alone in front of the TV. This is what my life has become, eating in front of the TV alone at home. But contrary to what I thought, I have got used to this new life, I even find a certain appeasement far from the madness of the world. Knowing that the people I like are having fun is enough for me. On the other hand, I miss cooking terribly. It is like a drug. I feel a crazy urge to cook, but as I cannot stand on my legs for very long, I can only prepare fast-made dishes. If Faith sees me in my kitchen, she gently orders me to sit down and continues to cook the dish I started.

She has not stopped impressing me. She takes care of me as if I were a kid and I have to say that it has been a long time since someone has taken care of me like that, without any hidden agenda, just to help. I am no longer a VIP, I am a human wreck, not very attractive. Her generosity of heart touches me enormously. I let go. Like a wild grizzly bear that has become a harmless teddy bear.

Our discussions sometimes took a more intimate turn. She told me about the devastating death of her husband. He was the love of her life, who passed away three years ago after a short battle with cancer. Her youngest offspring, a girl,

ɟ two at the time. They met in Kenya, an
.ıman from London working for a humanitarian
.nisation. She is still grieving, but has no choice but to
ɟ on with her life. Her six children need her. She works as
a housekeeper, out of necessity, as money is a bit scarce
without her husband's salary, but her real passion is
cooking.

I, of course, apologised many times for my behaviour of the
past, but she waved her hand, said that she understands I
was also kind of grieving after I told her about my love for
Marine and the pain in my heart.

Today, we are close. I am proud to say that she is my friend,
a true friend.

Watching her prepare delicious dishes in my kitchen gave
me an idea. Her meals are of course influenced by her
African culture. She uses spices imported from Zanzibar
previously unknown to me. And I must say that she cooks
like a goddess.

Therefore, I offered her to co-write my cookbook. After the
initial shock of my request, she quickly recovered and since
then we have spent one day a week trying out new recipes,
thinking, exchanging, experimenting, sharing opinions,
arguing, but the manuscript is progressing and I am very
happy about it.

Not as happy as she apparently, her son Oliver confided to
Gaston that his mother told the whole neighbourhood that
her cooking is so good that I have specially chosen her to

write my book with her. Which is true, but apparently impresses the suburbs.

The news also reached the very closed circles of the capital's VIPs and it seems to be widely commented on. The great chef Daniel writing his cookbook with his cleaning lady! Scandal! Their opinion does not interest me, I do not want to see these people anymore. These so-called friends have not called once since I fell ill, their silence is shattering. From now on I only want to be surrounded by people who have heart and not necessarily money.

❋

A while ago Gaston told me something that left me stunned: Boris and Benedict are in a relationship! Everybody knew it, except me. I worked for years with these two, I had them in front of my eyes almost every day and I never understood that they loved each other and will even tie the knot next year. How could I have been so blind? I recall my silly remark upon my return from Scotland about men kissing and not really being men. I still blush with shame at this. I was tired, I had spent a day in hell with the episode at Marcel's, but how could I have been so stupid?

I felt more than ashamed. I grabbed my phone, invited Boris and Benedict to my flat, to apologise for my attitude.

They do not seem to hold a grudge against me. Since then, Benedict visits me spontaneously. This guy is still a mystery to me, but I appreciate him. What I had taken for placidity is in fact a great listening capacity and humanity, accompanied by a touch of shyness. I gave him carte the new menu of vegetarian dishes. And since ...en cooking for me, I must say that his meals are surprises. I thought they were bland, tasteless, and , but it is the contrary. I find myself liking vegetarian ...isine more and more.

※

Gaston is under a lot of stress, I got him to replace me at the end of the year British Red Cross banquet, following the competition in the London-Bourg congress centre a few months ago. I sadistically put the pressure on him by saying that if he won the first prize, meaning being named best chef in the UK, I would make him a partner of The Yucca on a 50/50 basis. This almost made him cry, the emotion overwhelmed him.

But he soon came to his senses, said that he does not believe he will win, the competition is too high. The selected chefs are going to give the best of themselves during this evening. And Gaston, as he is replacing me, has to cook a Cambridgeshire dish. He thinks this is a disadvantage. I am not so sure, given his talent. Sometimes Gaston lacks self-confidence. But it is up to him alone to make his own experiences.

When he left me that day, he made a joke that we will not be partners before long.

He is very much mistaken. What he does not know is that I do not care if he wins or comes last. I have already consulted my solicitor and the documents are being drafted. I will hand them over to Gaston when he visits me in Stourpaine in January.

EPILOGUE

.on is shining from millions of light decorations. ople are flocking to the shopping centres to buy last-.ninute presents. Tomorrow, Christmas will be celebrated.

It is a beautiful winter day, although the cold is biting. My luggage is already in the trunk of Jake's car. My friend is waiting outside. I take a last look at my flat. I feel at the same time nervous and relieved. It is departure day to the health centre run by Damian.

When I turn the key in the lock, I tell myself that a chapter has just ended. For some time now I have been overwhelmed by these feelings of changing my life, of turning pages, of becoming another person.

A large silhouette is standing on the landing.

"Hi Daniel!".

"Hi Maxwell!".

Yes, my neighbour and I have become friends. Freed from my stress blindness, I saw beyond the bundle of muscles, I saw his big heart.

"You are escaping to the country! You are lucky! In any case, take care of yourself. Do not worry about your apartment, if a burglar tries to visit it, I will break their neck".

"Thank you, Maxwell, I am really lucky to have a neighbour like you. Enjoy the festive season! I do not know when I will be back, it will be up to the specialists at the centre to decide. Faith will keep you posted. I hope there will not be too much noise in January when the workers refurbish my flat. If that is the case, do not hesitate to give me a call, I will tell them to be more careful. And when I get back, I will organise a small gathering with Faith and Lloyd".

We shake hands warmly.

I press the button to call the lift up, a feeling of happiness comes over me. Like someone going on holiday, although I know full well that what awaits me is not exactly a holiday. I will have to talk frankly to the doctor, maybe to the psychologist, about what brings me to the centre. Medical exams, physical exercises, physiotherapy will follow. An unknown world.

Then in a few weeks' time, when I return, I will start working again. I am anxious about this; I have not worked for months. I have lost a bit of self-confidence and I am not sure I want to go back to the madness of life in the kitchen, the stress, the tensions, the arguments, the clients. What used to be my whole life, does not seem as important anymore, it even frightens me a bit.

Jake is going to drive me to Stourpaine in County Dorset, about 120 miles from London. This bucolic village has a population of no more than 800. It is situated on the River Stour in the middle of the countryside, at the moment frozen under snow and freezing cold. With Jake's car I wonder how long it will take us to reach the village. My friend is not known to respect speed limits. I bet that in less than two and ours we will be there, which will be more than ..1 to upset my back.

ourpaine seems to be exactly what I need at the moment, ..1 village atmosphere, clean air and country people. With a bit of luck, I will be fit enough to walk in the Hod Hills overlooking the village, from which the view seems to be magnificent.

In the car park I find my friend talking to Gaston. The latter with a broad smile holds out his hand and tells me that he wanted to wish me all the best. My throat tightens. I am touched. Since I opened my eyes, and my heart, I am sometimes overwhelmed by powerful positive emotions.

The engine noise of Jake's aerodynamic monster, my friend's beautiful car, is already humming. I do not know which one of us is more excited about this trip, him to show me the prowess of his jewel or me to finally get out of my daily life as a sick person enclosed between four walls. I am ready to get in the car, but I still have one last thing to settle.

And I finally dare to ask the question that has been bothering me for months and that made me almost go insane.

"Gaston, what is the mystery of your preparation of the Fendant sauce? It is exceptional!".

Gaston looks me straight in the eyes, a broad smile on his lips.

"There are no special ingredients. The secret is that I coo[k] with Love. In the last few years, you have forgotten to coo[k] with this amazing ingredient; Love".

❋

Gaston watches Jake's car taking Daniel to Stourpaine turning the corner.

He smiles.

Love, what nonsense! As if Love was enough to cook well!

Of course, he has not revealed his secret of making the Fendant sauce.

He saw them approaching with a huge smile and looking innocent. Jake launched the offensive, then Michael, then Florian, except Rick abstained. Even to his surprise, Benedict tried.

He did not flinch and did not utter a word. He created this recipe; it belongs to him. He will only reveal it when he deems it useful.

Competition is never far away among great chefs even if a sincere friendship unites them.

TO BE FOLLOWED......
Book 2: Chef Jake, *The Vegetables' Waltz*

ABOUT THE AUTHOR

.n Valais, in the south of Switzerland, in the French-
.ing minority, Mylène Thurre-Gex spent her childhood and
.nage years in the medieval village of Saillon. At the age of 19,
.o improve her language skills, she studied for a year in Bad-
Homburg (Germany), followed by two years in Brixton, London.

She then joined the International Committee of the Red Cross
(ICRC), where she carried out various missions in conflict zones,
including two years on the Thai-Cambodian border and a few
years between Iraq, Kenya and Somalia. She also worked at the
ICRC headquarters in Geneva. In 2011, after twenty years in the
humanitarian field, Mylène Thurre-Gex returned to her home
county.

Her marked interest in books began at a very young age by
reading comic strips. A graduate of Cambridge University UK,
Certificate of Proficiency in English, she has been passionate
about English literature since she was a teenager.

A convinced vegetarian, she currently lives in Valais and
continues to be involved in humanitarian work, as well as in the
protection and defence of animals.

Facebook: https://www.facebook.com/mylene.thurre.gex

Instagram: https://www.instagram.com/mylene_thurre_gex/?hl=fr

Also by Mylène Thurre-Gex

1. Le Chef Daniel, Le mystère de la sauce Fendant, 2017.

2. Le Chef Jake, La valse des légumes, 2017.

3. Le Chef Michael, Coralie, mon amour !, 2018.

4. Le Chef Rick, To be a Chef, or not to be a Chef, 2018.

5. Le Chef Florian, Une victime consentante, 2020.

6. Portraits, Personnalités de Saillon, 2021.

7. Le Velours, 2021.

8. En quête du bonheur !, 2022 (co-auteure).

9. Chef Daniel, The mystery of the Fendant sauce, 2022.

Printed in Great Britain
by Amazon

82197403R00139